MW01712332

GOSPELS OF THE NEW NILE

John Kilian

STRATTON
PRESS
Publishing Life

GOSPELS OF THE NEW NILE

Stratton Press Publishing
831 N Tatnall Street Suite M #188,
Wilmington, DE 19801
www.stratton-press.com
1-888-323-7009

ISBN (Paperback): 978-1-64895-320-0
ISBN (Ebook): 978-1-64895-321-7

Printed in the United States of America

This book is dedicated to all the parents who have lost children in the ongoing conflict between Islam and Christianity.

CONTENTS

PREAMBLE

Acknowledgments

For the inspiration to write, I am especially grateful to Okey Ndibe for taking time from his family and his writing to help me with my fledgling efforts. For the inspiration to care for the least among us, Manute Bol's life was marked by his dedication to improve the lives of his nation, whether in Sudan or in the United States.

Abbreviations

AT—After Temple, the number of years since the fall of the Third Temple
ERA—Ethiopian Regular Army
KU—Khartoum University
NEA—North Ethiopian Army
RC—Roman Census

Preface

This story was written before the Sudanese state was split in two, before the city of Abyei was razed by fire, and a decade before the damming of the Blue Nile in Ethiopia began construction. It was not written as an attempt to predict the future, far from it.

Politics and religion, throughout history, have served as a means of herding its flock to both the peaceable coexistence and the waging of war. Carnage and conciliation are always in the mix in the course of human relations.

The main purpose of this story is to give readers something they will enjoy reading. Any enlightenment gained, enabling a forecast of events to come, is a collateral, secondary effect and hopefully will not come at the expense of the pleasure that comes from reading an epic tale.

Izzi 3

Atonement

Throughout the Nile watershed, Passover was largely the same for all. When all had been assembled in the temple for the Passover celebration the clergy petitioned that all submit to the will of God as an act of subordination to the holy order of nature. It must have occurred to many if not most that subordination to nature and God should not include obedience to a regime of man-made instruction, but protests to the customs of the religion were unknown. With token consent from the congregation the temple doors were closed.

—*Book of Mysteries*
(From *The Book of the Great Passover*)

Captain Joseph's men formed a semicircle just outside the Blue Nile Tabernacle, assembling in the shade of the great structure before them. In Joseph's absence, Izzi stood in the leadership position at the focus of the company. He stroked his well-groomed beard before composing himself into a position of attention with both arms at his sides. Despite being the ranking man in the unit, it seemed strange to everyone to assemble before anyone other than their captain. "Fall in," he called out to the formation.

Echoes of scores of men snapping to attention bounced off the walls of the tabernacle and across the adjacent baptismal lagoon. Every tabernacle required a lagoon to supply water at the culmination of Passover. This water would wash away the sins of the congregation.

"Before we enter the tabernacle, the chaplain has some words he would like to share with us. Please give him your undivided attention." Izzi stepped back and was replaced by the uniformed chaplain, distinguished from the rest by his white belt.

The men remained at a rigid form of attention, while the chaplain took time to gather his thoughts. The bill of his uniform cap shaded his eyes, which were closed while he contemplated his next words. His fingers remained laced together until his eyes opened and he began to speak, "Behind us lies a lagoon of water, water made pure by the hand of God. This water in turn will purify this congregation. Behind us all lays a multitude of sins, which are a burden to our souls, and cause for worry at the time of atonement during Passover. But you have redeemed yourselves through your commitment to the Census and your bravery in the line of duty. That you have served God is now a matter of record. You have all received special markings upon returning from the wilderness. This should soothe your fears through the ordeal we all are about to face."

The assembled troops nodded in approval.

Izzi retook his post. "Front ranks first, file from the right," he commanded. The platoon guides turned over their right shoulder and relayed alternative commands of "circle right," and "stand fast," to their ranks. The men then marched in orderly arcs into the Blue Nile Tabernacle. Once inside, the special detachment of Census guards barred the only entrance shut from the outside.

Two by two, the men descended into darkness. They followed a spiral ramp until they reached the concentric pews that surrounded an altar bathed in sunlight from a glass dome above. Rising from incense burners into the atrium of the temple dome, smoke filled the room with a haze rich in opium.

The chaplain took his place in front of the altar, his white belt reflecting sunlight through the gathering haze. The onlookers stood on their feet to receive their cleric. He spoke without notes, panning the audience, fixing the gaze of every listener as he projected his words in calm tones, "We are gathered here to serve God in the faith that our world can survive only if humankind is willing to submit to the needs of the greater brotherhood of living things. We are saved by our belief that there is no greater cause and we are called to make the simplest sacrifice.

"In past times the tendency of people and nations to do as each saw fit left them with the least of liberty. People coveted one another's lands, and wars raged that left cities and whole countries in ruins. Divisions of people were drawn and redrawn along artificial boundaries that changed with the violent collisions of the states they contained."

He paused, taking the time to sip some water from a glass on the altar.

"Today, God's boundaries of water fallen from the heavens declares for us mere mortals where one nation begins and another ends. No nation need fear that their boundaries be erased by something as fickle as the imposing will of a neighbor. No other nation in the world would recognize the crime of conquest, and so there are no spoils of war to tempt one people to raise armies to attack another.

"Our swords are beaten into plowshares, and our fields are harvested in peace. We will not go hungry, as was so common in times gone past. When the harvest is made, there is food for all. We feel no need to hunt animals into extinction, or graze lands till they fail. What we have today, we will have tomorrow. There is no need to fear for our children's future. Our sacrifice today provides for those to come in our posterity.

"So much is provided us by yielding to the will of God. It is a small price we pay to fulfill the covenant of Passover. We offer ourselves for the greater good. We acknowledge the baptism to come as God's cleansing of our sins.

"None of us is without the blemish of humanity's fatal flaw. Does anyone not want more for himself or herself than what is possible to be shared by all? Who can claim to want less? Left to our own instincts, we fall prey to the ravages of selfishness that defines our original sin. We all sin. No one of us may be exempt from judgment. Some of us sin more than others, and we bear the markings of what we have taken from life and what we have given back. Not all of those who overly tax the land will be punished. Not all of us who sacrifice for others will be rewarded. The justice of Passover may seem flawed, as everything humans do truly is. But it is our attempts to please God and not deface the planet given us that is our saving grace. God gives us no certain instructions to save us from ourselves. We proceed from the darkness of the past to the salvation of the future saddled with doubts every step of the way. Assurance is found in the fruit of our ways. Knowing how we have failed in the past and seeing how we succeed in the present, is there anyone who doubts the path we follow is the way of the world?"

Rapt silence captured the congregation. The light against the billowing smoke cast a flowing shadow across the walls of the Tabernacle. "Hearing none, I now call for us all to submit to the accounting of sins. Those closest to the aisles may begin first..."

Captain Joseph's men displayed an orderliness and discipline that distinguished them from their past unruliness. They were all men with desperate histories who had followed their captain from Khartoum to the upper reaches of the Blue Nile, becoming new men in the transition.

Joseph's journey began before ever knowing any of the men that would come to revere him as their commander. In the Port of Aswan, far downstream of Khartoum, he began his journey from anonymity to greatness.

THE BOOK OF THE ASWAN

This is a story of love in days of the Great Passover. As is the case for all of the epics of the Holy Scriptures the truthfulness of this story cannot be ascertained through the acts of science. It is a story told without corroboration by written sources. The absence of any mention of the characters in the deciphered records surviving to this day make it both a treasure of the oral tradition and a challenge to one's faith. Indeed, this account is the product of the faithful, on whose lips alone it has been spoken over the centuries since the Great Passover, carried from generation to generation between the Founding Fathers and their blood kin.

Their account reveals to us many of the mysteries guarded closely in a time when secrecy was a matter of life and death. Knowledge of such matters as declared herein constituted treason in the time of their telling under the laws of the day. This is testament to the vigilance paid to the Holy Mysteries by its devotees in the centuries after the Great Passover.

—*Book of History*

Joseph 1

Three months before the Great Passover

Joseph, as the officer of the watch, began his entry in the duty log the way any centurion of the Roman Census would. "Day 23, Month 2 of the year 317 AT." While it was common to leave off the AT notation for "After Temple," centurions were expected to include it on official paperwork. It was as a reminder of the catastrophe that gave rise to the Census and the purpose for which it served.

He yawned and looked out over the locks of Aswan as he had so often before during his eighteen-month rotation. He checked the buttons of his uniform and found he had missed a hole. He wondered if he should bother fixing it. *Who in this place would care?* But he rebuttoned it anyway.

A fellow centurion entered the office, carrying a bottle. "Can I ask you a favor?"

Joseph smiled and shook his head. "Ali. You have a date tonight, don't you?" The man nodded. "Third time this month you've asked me to pull a double shift."

"Yes, well, lately there has been an increase in the number of women coming downstream. I figure, how long will it last?"

Lustful centurions contributed to Joseph's wealth. With each wave of new women, men came to him offering compensation to take their shifts. He personally preferred to spend his time without the palpable temptations of Nile women, but he played up the inconvenience of performing extra duty until his comrades offered the highest amount they could afford.

"As my relieving officer, there is a rule somewhere that says you are supposed to relieve me on a regular basis."

Ali met Joseph's eye. "But I wouldn't ask you to pull my shift if I didn't have a bottle of the best spirits to offer." Ali put the bottle beside the duty log.

"I'll be the judge of that." Joseph opened his locker and took out the hygrometer he used to gauge the quality of liquor. He estimated the value by determining the difference between its density and the density of pure, distilled water. He poured a sample from the bottle into the device, held it up to the light, taking its measure. After a routine pause, he turned to Ali with a grin and simply said, "Acceptable."

"Thank you, sir. As always, it has been an honor serving…" He left as quickly as he had arrived.

Time always seemed to pass slower the longer he worked, so he welcomed a distraction early on in his second shift of duty, The freighter *Terrier* arrived at the downstream lock at Aswan without notice or fanfare. Joseph received the captain in the narrow yet tidy office of the Census. Upon entering, the captain removed his cap, revealing his bald scalp. He tucked his cap under his arm and handed Joseph a series of documents. The ship's manifest included the list of passengers and crew, including their origin, destination, and the duration of their stay. Joseph perused the tables with the diligence of an auditor of the Roman Census.

"I see you have no immigrants to declare."

"This is true," the captain responded. "Just a crew and her cargo."

"Will you need quarters for the evening?" Joseph asked.

"I suppose I should be asking you if we have any need for quarters. Will it be necessary to delay our passage through the locks?" the captain replied.

"With no immigrants, it might not take all of three days," Joseph said, grinning.

The captain laughed. "I was hoping without immigrants we could pass through in three hours."

Joseph considered the request. *How badly does he want it?* he asked himself silently. With a slight grin, he asked, "Three hours is hardly time for a crew to enjoy the hospitality of Aswan." The glut of women at this checkpoint was legend.

"From what I hear, three hours in Aswan is enough time for any sailor to enjoy her hospitality. And that is why I intend to quarantine the crew during our ascent through the locks."

At this, both men roared with laughter. Joseph thought this captain something of a character to deny his crew liberty call in a place where sailors craved the shortest of leaves. "Obviously, you are not a captain in fear of mutiny?"

The captain smiled, but didn't respond. He was intent on getting this business done as soon as possible.

The pregnant pause lingered as Joseph considered his options. It occurred to him that time was on his side, and he decided to draw out the matter to enhance his position in the negotiations. "I will need to see the cargo manifest."

The captain barely concealed his hostility to the centurion's mandate. This was an unusual request for a checkpoint halfway up the Nile. "I cleared watershed customs in Alexandria, and I have no new cargo to declare."

"The Census has no desire to delay you unnecessarily," Joseph countered, underlining the notion that he and he alone represented the Roman Census and reserved the right to exercise all its bureaucratic processes as he saw fit. "It is simply a matter that to be fair, I need to be thorough with all ships passing through these locks."

"And I want to be fair with you, sir. Would it expedite matters if I were to unload a parcel of undocumented cargo before my ship clears these locks?"

"It very well might. What is the undocumented cargo?"

The captain withdrew a leather purse and placed it on the Joseph's desk. "Just this."

Joseph casually untied the cinches of the purse, which itself was of considerable value by virtue of it being made of animal skin. He gazed down at the contents of the purse and then met the look of the captain, speechless.

"Don't spend it all in one place," the captain chided.

"I am not sure I could spend it all in one place."

The captain nodded. Joseph nodded as well, processed the papers, and handed them back.

Jasmine 1

Three months before Great Passover

Jasmine was typical of the women applying to immigrate below Aswan. She was dark in complexion, wore a veil across her face, and cared for her pet cat like it was her own child. She held few possessions, a reflection of her status as a virtual refugee.

Every year the Nile Protocol, the ultimate law of the land, required more and more territory of the upper Nile to be laid fallow to ensure the integrity of the water supply to the downstream community and to preserve the sustainability of the soil in lands overworked by the settlers of the upper Nile.

As was the case with any female citizen, she was eligible to take a husband in and downstream of her native watershed. In this way, the Nile Protocol was the same as the protocols of all the great waterways. All observed the Ethic of Sovereign Watersheds: God divided land in the same way He divided Man. Water did not range from watershed to watershed, and so neither should the blood of Man. And so the political boundaries of the civilized world were in commune with those of nature, and Man obeyed the boundaries set by nature and God.

The Nile Protocol had been gradually depopulating the component watersheds above Khartoum. The Ethic of Sovereign Watersheds allowed an egress downstream for the women of the condemned territories. Men, however, were not provided with the same freedoms. A man had to take a wife who was born at or above his native watershed. When the Nile Protocol began declaring reserves in upstream territories, the men faced rigid restriction on emigration. A man wed legally to a woman of his watershed could generally pass downstream at will. Of course, few women wished to make their way down the Nile hindered by a marriage to a landless groom. Since few men above Khartoum had the resources to acquire downstream real estate, few succeeded in gaining the hand of the women of their homeland. Depopulation brought many a woman to annul her marriage so that she could seek the plentiful dowry of a downstream groom. Under the Nile Protocol, such desperate acts were necessary for a woman to ensure her survival, and that of her children.

As Jasmine sat in the dormitory provided her during her stay in Aswan, she considered the rebirth that would come again to her homeland. "Mine is a small burden to bear to bring about the resurrection of the Nile," she canted to her companion, Cleopatra. Cleopatra met the gaze of her mistress and reflected the adoration with a deep and rhythmic purr. Jasmine petted the black fur coat of her cat while she recited her prayers. She fell asleep praising the will of God.

Joseph 2

Joseph secured the leather bag in his personal locker as soon as the captain vacated the customs office. He then went to the window and gazed down on the ship like a beneficiary looking on the coffin of some unknown uncle. He was grateful for the windfall from this stranger, and curious of the purpose behind this good fortune.

He peered down on the deck of the *Terrier* and saw nothing of note. Rigging, crew, and cargo all appeared perfectly normal, and yet he thought it impossible that a vessel carrying what must be extraordinary cargo should appear as any other. He looked on in a trance as the first lock flooded, slowly hoisting the ship to the second level. Then he began to sense something was abnormal about this boat.

Joseph frequently watched the ships passing his checkpoint, daydreaming about the faraway ports these ships would visit. His lengthy meditations while viewing these ships in the lock emblazoned in his memory a subconscious template of what a ship in a lock looked like. This ship was different. A difference so subtle that it might go unnoticed in river water or open ocean was made obvious in the oxygenated waters that passed through these locks, like standing white water. In this less dense water, the *Terrier* sank lower than any vessel he had ever seen passing this busy port of call. Whatever there was on board this ship, it obviously was of incredible weight.

Joseph returned to his personal locker where he had just secured his latest bribe. He removed from it the hygrometer and walked down to the lock and sampled the density of the bubbling waters swirling about the *Terrier*. He made note of the depth at which the freighter floated and then computed the weight of the volume of water it displaced.

What is this freighter hauling, rocks? What could be worth such an overwhelming bribe to conceal?

He spent the remainder of his shift watching the vessel rise from lock to lock until it reached the level of the Nile above Aswan and set off into the distance.

Jasmine 2

Jasmine awoke at dawn and performed her morning prayer ritual before breakfast. Cleopatra jumped up on the breakfast table and joined her for a bowl of oatmeal. "You seem to be in a rush today. Do you have an important appointment to keep?" The cat ignored the question in favor of cleaning the bowl of any leftover food.

She gathered together her personal documents and stored them in a coarse saddlebag that acted as her purse. It had been passed down for generations to her from the time before cattle were banned from the Blue Nile. The antique saddlebag was all she had to remind her of her home far up the Blue Nile, above Khartoum and to the east. All she knew was now a preserve, home to grass and trees and water pure, but void of her kinsmen, or any other people, for that matter, except for centurions keeping vigil and pocketing diamonds from time to time when they encountered the rare stranded soul who had chosen to defy the Nile Protocol.

With all her documents in order, she picked up her feline and placed it in the other empty saddlebag and slung the pouches over her shoulder. She shifted the straddle strap to balance the load between the documents in the rear bag and the cat in the front one. Cleopatra's head emerged from within the satchel and mildly meowed in protest. "Be good, kitten. You know how you hate it when I have to leave you behind." She cinched down a flap to enclose the cat in the carrier and, after drawing her veil across her face, left her dormitory.

She crossed the green between the dormitory and the Census House at a brisk pace, anxious to conclude her immigration process and begin a new life. At the gate to the Census House, she paused to read the inscription on the archway above, "In God We Trust."

Yes, she thought, *I must not fear for my placement. My destination is deemed by God.* Quickly she climbed the stairway and passed down the hallway to the Office of Naturalization.

She was ten minutes early for her appointment. The officer she was to meet was fifteen minutes late. To pass the time, she continued her prayers where she had left off the night before. It had a soothing effect, as did the purring of her cat in the saddlebag on her lap.

When the immigration officer arrived, she rose awkwardly from her seat in a sign of deference. The man smiled at the gesture. "Please, remain seated. I am your humble servant," he said with his right palm on his heart. His words and gesture were repeated often in the course of his duties, as routine as opening a door to let another to enter ahead of you as a courtesy.

She blushed slightly in mild embarrassment and took comfort in the man's kind words. He unlocked the door to his inner office and invited her in, holding the door open to allow her to pass before him. He closed the door behind him and walked around his desk. She stood waiting until the man smiled again, "Please, be seated. Make yourself comfortable."

The two seated themselves. "Now, all I know about you right now is that you are a charming lady from the Blue Nile and you wish to emigrate below Aswan."

"Yes, sir. This is correct," she replied curtly.

"Well, of course I must know more about you than this." He looked at her with eyes open with surprise that he needed to state the obvious..

"Oh, of course! Let me give you my documents." She uncinched the saddlebag holding the documents and produced several neatly rolled scrolls tied with colored ribbons. The immigration officer received the scrolls with a nonplus expression and ordered them on his desk according to color. The first scroll he opened, tied with green ribbon, was an interdepartmental form which simply designated the time and place of the meeting taking place.

"Your name is Jasmine."

"Yes."

"Mine is Martin." They nodded to one another as a formality.

The second scroll, bound with black ribbon, was her birth certificate. Martin made a few notations on his ledger, glancing back and forth between the scroll and the ledger. "You have come a long way. Life is very different below the cataracts."

She did not respond, but looked puzzled.

Martin looked at her and smiled weakly. "Jasmine, are you aware that it is not the custom of women below the cataracts to wear veils in private meetings? Perhaps you would like to unveil yourself? If only to make our meeting less formal."

She was caught off guard by the request. She did not consider this to be a private engagement, and this man, although friendly, was a perfect stranger. Nevertheless, she complied, removing her veil and exposing her face to a strange man for the first time in her life. With the veil clumsily tucked into her blouse pocket, she sensed herself to be more vulnerable than before.

"Such a beautiful face. It seems to me almost a sin to hide God's good work."

She nodded again and pondered his words. She had been raised to believe such exposure to be sinful. The morals of the lower Nile would be difficult to accept.

A blue ribbon was tied around a third scroll. It enclosed her application for immigration, and it was much longer than the black or green scrolls. "This will take a while for me to digest. Feel free to make yourself at home. There is coffee ready in the cooler, if you would like," he said pointing to a small brown box in the corner of the office to his right.

"Thank you. Would you care for some yourself?"

"If you wouldn't mind, Jasmine, I would like a dash of cream with mine."

Her pupils dilated slightly at the mention of the word *cream*. Animal husbandry was a thing of the past in her homeland. Of course, she knew from accounts that cows were still raised downstream. She rose from her seat, leaving the saddlebags on the chair, and walked to the cooler. She opened the lid and peered down on the carafes of coffee and cream. This was the first time she had actually seen a dairy product, despite the fact that her ancestors drove cattle across the watershed of the Blue Nile for generations. She poured the coffee into a pair of ceramic cups set on saucers on a shelf just above the cooler. She decided to add the cream to her coffee as well as to his. When she was done pouring, she brought the man his coffee.

"Thank you, Jasmine. I can tell you must be an excellent hostess." This was high praise for a woman of her upbringing. Hosting was considered a great measure of character in her native culture.

"You can tell so much from the way I pour coffee?" she exclaimed in surprise.

Martin laughed heartily, thinking it a jest. "Jasmine, do you know how rare it is for me to enjoy a sense of humor in the course of my duties? You bring a special warmth to these cold walls."

She felt warmth in the cheeks of her face and wished her veil was still attached to her dress. "You are too kind."

"Martin. Please call me Martin. And I think you will find the couch by the cooler is a more comfortable place to drink coffee than your chair."

She saw that on either end of the couch there were shelves where she could set her coffee between sips. She placed her coffee on a shelf and sat in the well-cushioned couch. "Thank you, Martin." She found the couch much more comfortable than the chair, although she did not feel comfortable calling this man by his first name. She spied the saddlebags left on her chair, wondering if Cleopatra would be okay cinched in a sack without her near.

After a few minutes of review, Martin looked up from the scroll. "Your request betrays your ambition. A placement in a university is a much-coveted prize."

She was somewhat shaken by the inference that her request was excessive. "My understanding is that compensation for being displaced from a preserve would give me some preference in selection by downstream universities."

"Yes, Jasmine, your understanding of the Nile Protocol is accurate, in this respect. But you need to appreciate that Nile politics come into play when university appointments are at stake."

"Politics?"

"Beneath the cataracts, there are as many fine universities as there are subpar institutions. A resumé with the former on it can open doors to a splendid career. With only a subpar university to your name, many of these doors seal shut. A person's dreams and ambitions rest not on whether they attend university, but which one they attend."

"I see." Her voice was aquiver. She shrank into her corner of the couch and dropped her gaze to her clenched hands.

Martin, seeing her troubled expression, rose from his chair and approached the couch carrying his coffee. "Relax, Jasmine. These things are reason for concern but not for worry." He sat on the cushion beside her and put his coffee on the shelf beside.

"Oh, please, Martin. I do so much want to be a geologist. This might be the only way I can return to my homeland." She looked at him with eyes ready to shed tears.

Martin put his arm around her, and she found solace in his comforting gesture. He let out a sigh and stared ahead blankly. After a few moments, she turned to him, begging, "Martin, is there something you can do for me?"

"My dear Jasmine. Of course there is, but first I must ask, isn't there something you can do for me?"

Joseph 3

The spartan surroundings of Joseph's billet included the staple furniture afforded soldiers in the Roman Census: a stiff bed, a coarse duffel, a lamp, and a stone floor. Not that more comforts would make Joseph any less restive, but the barren environment of his residence did add urgency to his will to leave this place in favor of new lands. He awoke well after sunrise the morning after pulling his most profitable double shift. Despite his lack of belongings, in general, it still took him a few minutes to put together a suitable off-duty wardrobe. With no known potential visitors to see the inside of these quarters, their upkeep lapsed entirely until the point that everything Joseph owned was scattered at random.

Whatever order his quarters lacked, his front yard garden epitomized tidiness. Concentric rows about a water pool were divided into equal quadrants. From a central reservoir, water coursed down through the rows and the four channels connecting them, delineating each of the quadrant boundaries. Joseph had realized his vision of a garden that needed no hand-watering and imagined future tenants of his quarters appreciating his cleverness as well as the garden itself. *All one leaves behind is their influence.*

His garden was perhaps the solitary entity that held meaning for him. He could always look at it and feel a sense that he had accomplished something of lasting beauty and grace. And if his garden was the lone signature of his personal merit, the garden preserves held a similar status for the Roman Census. Despite the wanton corruption and partisan patronage with which the Census was inured, it did serve to accomplish a sacred mission. So long as the Census remained vigilant, the preserves would bloom forever.

For breakfast, he picked the largest of the ripe tomatoes and ate it on his way to meet with his commander. As he passed the gate to the Census House, he noticed again the inscription: "In God We Trust."

And in diamonds, too, he thought.

A set of stone stairs led to the outer door of the detachment headquarters. Joseph passed through the unlocked door and entered the floral atrium that served to impress entrants to the facility with nature's brilliance captured in miniature. The orderly was watering the beds by hand. This was the archetypal chore of an underling in the Census.

Joseph recalled a superior's reprimand he received early in his career, "Keep your bearing when you are in uniform, or you will be watering daisies in Africa."

Joseph regained the confidence of his superior but had never forgotten these words of caution.

"Orderly, is the commander in?"

"Yes, sir."

"I need you to witness a formal request. Please follow me." The orderly followed the officer to their commander's office. The pair walked past a mural of a river banked by forests. At the far end of the mural, an open doorway led to the commander's office.

"Come in, by all means. What can I do for you, Joseph?"

"Not to waste words, sir, I have come to request a transfer."

The commander raised his eyebrows. Joseph knew himself to be one of the more reliable officers and that his commander would be unhappy about losing him.

"Why? And to where?" he asked.

"It is not a matter I take lightly, sir. This command has been good to me. It is just that I have six months left on the Nile, and I hope to see more of it than Aswan in that time."

The commander nodded. He could not think of a reasonable counter that might lead his man to stay. "You have been good for this command, but all good things must come to an end. Where do you wish to transfer?"

Joseph's face relaxed, releasing the tension that had been sustained all morning in anticipation of resistance to his request. "I am looking for time on the frontier. Whether Blue or White, I am not decided."

"I see. May I offer a suggestion?"

"Yes, sir."

"In Khartoum, you can see the Blue and the White."

Jasmine 3

"*My dear Jasmine. Of course there is, but first I must ask, isn't there something you can do for me?"*

Before Jasmine could do more than shrink away from Martin's hot gaze, Cleopatra let a bloodcurdling meow from her confinement. Jasmine slid out of Martin's embrace and ran to her saddlebags. She scooped her cat up and held her close, soothing the agitated animal in her arms.

Martin stood slowly, his cheeks flushed. He stumbled in his speech, searching for new words that could rejuvenate his chase. "A cat. You have brought your cat?" he chortled in false humor that she took as a form of condescension. He maneuvered across to the huddled pair in feigned nonchalance. Stretching out his hand awkwardly, he spoke in suggestive tones, "May I pet your little cat?"

The cat hissed, and spit, and threatened to scratch the man closing in. Jasmine trembled. This was a strange reaction for Cleopatra. She held her closer, whispering calming words. Recoiling from the ugliness of the animal's reaction, the man stepped back and momentarily lapsed into a look of disbelief. He managed to suggest gently, "If you restored your pet to its holder, perhaps we can finish our coffee."

She heard the voice of a parent in the man and sensed more fully the perversity of his intent. With obvious contempt ringing in her words as revulsion welled up inside of her, she replied, "I am finished drinking my coffee."

He returned to his side of his desk. "Unfortunately, my dear, I am not finished with your paperwork."

Joseph 4

The captain would surely have slept through the afternoon had it not been for the urgency of Joseph to leave Aswan far, far behind. Joseph caught the man in his slumber with his feet resting on the steering wheel and his eyes sewn shut by the gentle rocking of the boat beneath him.

"Excuse me."

The mariner stirred, caught off guard, and stumbled to his feet. As he emerged from the darkened cabin, the bright light of the noon sun dilated his pupils of his age-strained eyes. Eventually the mirage before him sharpened into focus, and his stooped frame straightened in the presence of a centurion officer. While made anxious by the mysterious appearance of a man of authority, the elderly captain felt relieved that the strange voice he heard emanating from the blurry aberration on the sun-drenched deck did indeed have a human face to go with it.

"Sir, how may I be of service?"

"You are the captain of this ship?"

"Yes, sir. Captain Israel. Welcome aboard the *Pursuit of Happiness*."

"Then this is for you." Joseph removed a folded document from his shirt pocket and handed it to the ship's captain.

Captain Israel received the document and recognized it as an order for transport. He frowned as he verified the authenticity of the command, a look of wonder overtaking his facial expression. "I am at your service," he replied finally.

"When does your ship sail?"

"We'll be ready at a moment's notice, sir."

"If that means by sunset, I'll be happy."

Jasmine and Joseph 1

The office of the harbormaster of the Aswan lagoon was a petite, tidy shack overlooking the man-made inlet carved out of the Nile above the first cataract. From its perch, the flow of vessels to and from the lagoon could be observed, as well as the channels that coursed through the ruins of the ancient Aswan Dam. In addition to managing lagoon traffic, it was the duty of the harbormaster to monitor these channel depths and warn ships straying too close to the Aswan shoals.

Upon entering this office, Joseph was struck by the contrast between the occupants of the tiny shelter. On his left, an older man in the uniform of the harbormaster dutifully stood staring over the lagoon and the channels in the distance, his eyes hidden completely by thick dark sunglasses. On his right sat a young woman in civilian dress, her face veiled so that the only part of her visible were her eyes, and she stared downward at the shaded stone floor, as if to hide from the light of day. She sat on a rigid wooden bench with a leather saddlebag straddled across her lap, one hand curiously set inside on of the pouches.

"Good afternoon, sir. How can the Harbormaster's Office be of service?"

"I am here to register the departure of the *Pursuit of Happiness*."

"Captain Israel's boat?"

"Aye, aye."

"This is a military transport?"

"It is."

"Well, it is about time 'Old Channel Runner' earned his pay. Are you headed up or downstream?"

"Upstream."

The harbormaster opened the smaller of two logs where entries were made for departures downstream and upstream, respectively. "And for where are you and the good captain bound?"

"Khartoum."

The heretofore-oblivious younger woman joined the older man in a look of surprise. "That is a great distance on a small boat," the harbormaster stated frankly.

"A centurion doesn't need a lot of room for luggage."

"Neither does this daughter of the Blue Nile."

Joseph turned to the woman seated on the bench and was met with a sheepish look. "You are headed to Khartoum?" Joseph asked.

She did not answer, but only looked away. Joseph was taken aback by her reaction to his question and returned his gaze to the harbormaster.

"That would depend on the availability of upstream bound vessels," he offered in her absence. "As you might notice, my upstream departure log is a slender volume. It could be weeks before a commercial carrier can take her to Khartoum at the price she can afford. Your vessel is not large, but it is seaworthy. Certainly, there is room for a third."

Out of the corner of his eye, Joseph noted his would-be co-traveler wore a look of concern. He turned to her again. "You are in a rush to get to Khartoum?"

"I am anxious to leave Aswan, but I am not willing to offer more than a third rate fare."

"I understand. Of course, you do not have to haggle with me. It is not my boat, and I am not authorized to amend the manifest signed by my commander."

She looked at the stone floor.

"No one is suggesting she be listed as military personnel," the harbormaster spoke with authority. "But your craft is a commercial charter. Its captain can choose his crew."

"I cannot speak for Captain Israel."

"But I can. Khartoum is a long journey. The captain will surely take her on as a much-needed mate."

"How can you be sure?"

"You mean, how can *you* be sure?"

"I'm sorry…?"

"Were you planning on clearing port anytime soon?"

The centurion now felt the leverage of authority over him in the way he had wielded his authority over ship's captains many times before. "I understand that it is customary for a ship's captain to present his harbormaster with a bottle of spirits upon departing his home port."

"Unfortunately, your captain's choice of beverage does no honor to this tradition."

"What is your pleasure, sir? I am sure I can intervene on my captain's behalf."

"Only the finest kind."

"I will return shortly."

"Not necessary. Simply take this woman with you and inform him that his services in employing her are welcomed in lieu of a departure gift for the harbormaster."

Joseph recognized there was no room for negotiation on this point. "Very well." Joseph turned to her. "Can I help you with your belongings?"

"I am carrying them now, thank you." She turned to the harbormaster. "Thank you, sir. I cannot repay you for your charity."

"If you repaid me, miss, then it would not be charity."

The three-man crew cast off and soon entered the channel leaving the Aswan lagoon. Under the watch of the harbormaster, the vessel soon cleared the last of the channel markers. Before turning upstream, Joseph saw a series of flags fly up the flagpole in the distance, above the harbormaster's office. He moved from the stern to the helm where the captain was face forward, guiding his boat through the last of the channel. "Captain, a semaphore message is being sent by the harbormaster."

"In the clear?"

"I am not certain."

"'Not certain'?"

"I can't decipher semaphores."

"Oh, they don't teach soldiers semaphores anymore? Take the wheel and hold her steady till I get back." The aged captain shuffled to the stern and raised a spyglass toward the shore. After several minutes of recording semaphores, the captain took up a pair of handheld flags and signaled a few characters to confirm receipt of the message. He then stowed the glass and the flags and returned to the helm of his craft.

Once relieved of the steering wheel, Joseph turned to the captain, "What was the message?"

"The harbormaster told us to 'Take good care of Cleopatra.'"

Joseph turned to the first mate. "I thought your name was Jasmine?"

Jasmine smiled without answering and reached into her saddlebag, where a fourth crewmember stowed away.

THE BOOK OF THE TRANS-KHARTOUM

Israel 1

After clearing the last channel markers, Captain Israel came about, setting a tack aimed directly at the ruins of the ancient Aswan Dam. "This isn't the fastest way upstream, but it is worth the scenery to lose an hour."

"Scenery?" Joseph wondered aloud.

"From this distance, the dam remnants look like so much antique rubble. But when you see them close up, you appreciate the majesty of pre-Temple construction."

Intrigued, Joseph fixed his gaze on the horizon. The cement structure grew larger as they approached. A set of orange buoys floating in a line perpendicular to the boat's path became visible. Joseph unrolled a chart of the waters around Aswan and found the orange symbols on it that mapped the location of the orange buoys. He noticed they created a line parallel and slightly downstream of the Aswan Dam ruins. The word "*foul*" was written on the chart upstream of the line. He reviewed the chart's legend and found the orange symbol listed as a warning buoy.

The boat continued to approach the dam ruins, but Joseph was no longer focused on the ever-enlarging monument towering above the Nile. Instead, he was now fixated on the proximity of the orange buoys.

"Captain, should we prepare to come about?" His face was taut with concern, and his eyes were wide with surprise as they progressed to within a few boat lengths of the buoy line.

"No." The captain's voice was low and slow, with a hint of annoyance. The brevity belied his absolute authority over the movements of his vessel. No explanation was necessary for any decision he made.

Jasmine, who had been staring at the marvel of masonry rising more than a hundred cubits above the level of the water, turned towards the two men. She frowned slightly at the formality and terseness of their exchange. She looked at the orange buoys and surmised correctly that they were the source of this soft-spoken conflict. "What are these orange buoys here for?" she asked.

The captain did not reply. Instead he minded his rudder and sail, all the while gazing into the distance.

After having given Israel a fair chance to answer, Joseph replied, "They are warning buoys."

"Warning? Is there some danger?" She gathered Cleopatra into her arms. She looked towards Joseph; Joseph turned to Israel; and Israel turned his head over his left shoulder at a patch of eddying water a boat length away.

"Don't worry about the chart, Joseph. I've been this way a dozen times before, I assure you. Just keep an eye starboard for any eddies. They will tell us where the rocks are."

"Rocks? In the middle of the Nile?" Jasmine piped.

"Remnants of the dam, my dear. Blown to smithereens in the war of the Third Temple. That monolith of cement ahead is just a small fraction of the dam that held back the waters of the Nile further than the eye could see." The captain spun the wheel hard to the left and trimmed the sail rapidly. "Jasmine, could you go to the front of the boat and keep an eye out for swirling water? And stow your cat below deck, please."

Jasmine reacted instantly, putting her feline into her saddlebag and lowering it into the cargo hold. Then she took up a position ahead of the forward mast. Within a few minutes, she spotted a blemish in the otherwise smooth surface of the water. A post protruded out of the water. "Captain, there is something standing in the water ahead of us!"

"Come about!" Israel bellowed as he spun the wheel frantically to the right. Joseph ducked low to avoid the sail swinging across the deck. The boat leaned hard on its keel to the right, and Cleopatra wailed as the saddlebag she was in slid across the floor of the hold. The rudder of the vessel lifted out of the water from being on such a sharp angle, and the boat drifted, out of control of the helm, towards the obstacle.

"All hands to port!" he yelled.

Joseph and Jasmine scrambled to the left side of the boat, and the boat leveled enough for the rudder to sink below the water. As the nose of the boat turned to the right, a wooden post rising out of the water stood half a boat length to the left.

"What is that?" Joseph asked.

"That, Joseph, is the mast of the *Spartan*."

"A wreck?" He looked at the chart briefly. "There are no known wrecks on the chart. How are you so sure this is the *Spartan*?"

"Because the *Spartan* used to be my boat."

Once beyond this obstacle, Israel set course on a line a few degrees to the left of the ruins. "You can relax, now. We are past the rocks and the wrecks." The crew released audible sighs, and Jasmine rushed to the hold and released Cleopatra.

"Captain?" she asked.

"Aye."

"Of the dozen times you came this way, how many times did your ship sink?"

Joseph's head reared back in a silent laugh, while Israel gave a sheepish grin at his own expense. Now clear of the swirling currents that eddied around grave obstacles, the captain's furrowed brow smoothed. It was as if the man's face reflected the nature of the water on which he sailed. In the raging channel through the dam ruins, his face contorted as violently as the water around him. His voice, too, was staccato with an edge of anger while barking orders here and there. Once reaching safer waters, his expression and tone turned placid. "Only the one time, the first time I came this way. After that, I knew how to avoid trouble," he replied.

"But why would you risk your boat coming this way in the first place?"

"Well, you see, I always knew the channel we are in, now, had to exist. There is too much water coming this side of the ruin for it not to cut a channel."

"So you were curious enough to risk your boat?"

"That, and the fact that I had the Census on my ass."

Joseph roared in laughter. The captain's off-color remark told him that he was at liberty to address him as a peer. "I take it you had something to hide?"

"A full load of contraband coffee to hide. And I hid it where no Census inspector is ever going to find it, under thirty feet of water."

Jasmine's eyebrows rose high. "You were smuggling?"

Israel hunched his shoulders and shook his head side to side. "No, ma'am. I wouldn't call it smuggling. I was merely delivering goods directly to a recipient and avoiding any delay that might occur by stopping at customs."

Joseph, who had been smiling throughout Jasmine's quiz of the captain, stopped long enough to speak. "I am glad you cleared that up, Israel. For a moment there, I thought you might have been smuggling."

The boat passed into the shadow of the remnants of the dam. The sails lufted as the breeze diminished in the vicinity of the remaining shield of cement. Joseph and Jasmine craned their necks to keep the top of the structure in view.

"Why would anyone build a dam this large? It must have killed a good deal of what lived in the river," Jasmine said.

"Of course," Joseph added.

Israel pursed his lips before answering. "The dam supported agriculture that fed millions. It provided electricity to people, as well."

"How did they ever get along without it?" Joseph's words dripped with sarcasm.

"They didn't," Israel countered. "After the dam was destroyed in the War of the Temple, people began to starve. The Passover ritual was created as a means to trim the herd, so to speak."

Jasmine pulled her cat close and stared at Israel with eyes wide and unblinking. Joseph dipped his gaze down to the deck before looking up and asking, "You seem to know a good many things that aren't common knowledge."

"I know the truth, and the truth is seldom common knowledge."

Jasmine put her cat down. "I would like to hear more."

The captain recounted the events that led to the destruction of the dam. The building of the Third Temple on the site of the Second Temple required the razing of Al Aqsa, an Islamic shrine. The ensuing conflict escalated to include nuclear, biological, and chemical weapons of mass destruction.

Jasmine hung on his every word while Joseph stared off into the distance. It seemed as if the deck of the boat had been transformed into a university lecture hall where half the class listened intently and half could not be bothered. When the captain had finished telling how the rise and fall of the Third Temple had led to the Great War, Jasmine asked, "But what does any of this have to do with Passover?"

Israel turned to her, but kept Joseph in his peripheral vision. "In the war, people downstream of here took to shelters beneath ground, hoping to survive the bombs incinerating the world above. There wasn't room for everyone, so lots were drawn to determine quickly who would enter the shelter and who would not. The shelters were made as airtight as possible for fear the air would be made poison."

"How does the air become poison?" Jasmine asked.

At this, Joseph turned from staring into the distance towards her and said, "The ancient world had untold means of undoing all that comes beautiful in the natural world."

"Yes," Israel added. "That is all very true. But it wasn't air, of course, that kills people in Passover, then or now. When it was breached, a wall of water as high as the dam flowed downstream. That water passed over the people in the better-built shelters, and so they survived. Those in shelters that weren't quite watertight drowned in the flood."

Joseph's attention was now fixed on the captain. "The first Passover was an accident?"

"Aye. When the survivors came aboveground, they discovered a ruined world. The lands once irrigated by waters held back by the dam soon dried up and were reclaimed by the desert. When the mourning of the dead was over, they realized that there would not have been food enough to feed everyone had there not been so many killed. The ritual of Passover began with people thanking God that their neighbors had drowned."

Jasmine sat silently, looking down at Cleopatra as she petted her long black fur. Joseph looked at Israel for a while. When the boat left the shadow of the dam, the breeze picked up. The captain pulled in the sail and steered towards the south and upstream. Once the rigging was fixed for the new setting, Joseph looked towards his captain and said, "History is filled with bad stories, isn't it, old man?"

Israel 2

The captain broke off his tack and headed for the western shore.

"Are we going ashore, Captain?" Joseph asked.

"Aye."

"Is there a problem?" Jasmine asked, her brow wrinkling slightly.

"Just going to take on water at a nearby well."

"Water? But we've barely left port?" Joseph cried, as much in surprise as anything.

"Always good to top off, Joe. We are heading south, after all." When they were within a handful of boat lengths from the dock, Israel turned his craft into the wind to slow their approach.

"Jasmine, would you please ready the line on the stern? Joseph, could you take the bow?"

"Aye."

"Aye." They both darted to their respective cleats and made ready to dock.

"Be careful stepping onto the dock."

"Not to worry, Captain, though it is nice to know you care." A smile crept across Joseph's face as he hopped from the boat to the rickety planks of the dock. The impact of the leap made the wooden dock creak and moan.

"I am more worried about the dock." Israel turned to the stern and caught Jasmine smiling uncontrollably.

On shore, Israel led them, carrying two large bladders over his back. Jasmine brought her saddlebag and her cat. Joseph walked along with a rope wrapped around his right shoulder. Israel looked ahead, eyes wide like a child opening gifts on his birthday. "This is a special well, my friends."

Jasmine hustled to keep up with Israel's brisk pace. "Special, how so?"

"This well is on the Tropic of Cancer."

"The what?" Jasmine asked, frowning.

"This is the furthest north that sunlight shines directly on the earth."

"The sun doesn't shine directly down on Aswan?"

The captain shook his head from side to side. "No, ma'am, it does not."

"How do you figure?"

"Have you ever seen the bottom of a well in Aswan?"

She pouted out her lower lip. "No."

"And you never will. That is because Aswan is north of the Tropic of Cancer, and the sun does not shine straight down to the ground north of the Tropic of Cancer, where we are standing right now."

The captain got on his knees and put the bladders on the ground. He ran his fingers through the dirt, uncovering an iron handle. He swept away more dirt to reveal an iron panel. He swung it open, and the rusted hinges let out a metallic yawn. Joseph extended to him an end of the rope, and he fastened a knot to one of the bladders. He guided the rope clear of the edge of the well, as Joseph fed him more line, unwrapping it from his shoulder.

Only a few loops of line were left when water was finally reached. "The water is low." The second bladder was lowered and raised. "When the water is low, the Passover runs high, does it not?"

Joseph replied, "When there is less water, fewer can be allowed to drink. Passover is a harsh thing, but it saves us all from starving."

Israel untied the rope from the second bladder. "Since I brought these up, you two can bring them down."

On the boat, Jasmine lit a lantern as the sun set across the river. "Captain, why is there a well way out here in the middle of nowhere?"

"That well is three thousand years old, and this, at one time, at least, used to be the middle of somewhere. And on top of that, there is the business of this being on the Tropic of Cancer, after all." He rewound the rope and fastened it to a cleat on the deck.

Joseph and Jasmine exchanged looks of puzzlement. "Why is that important?"

"Three thousand years ago, that very well was used to measure the earth. On the first day of summer, light at noon reaches to the bottom of this well. In the delta to the north, however, it does not."

Joseph yawned. "So you have said before."

Jasmine sat up. "Yes, you said this before, but what does this have to do…"

"It has to do with everything. The angle of the light in the delta on the first day of summer, combined with the knowledge of the distance from this well to the delta, can be used to calculate the circumference of the Earth. Three thousand years ago, Africans determined this, using this very well."

Jasmine stayed silent for a while. "Circumference?"

Joseph picked up an orange. "An old Latin term for the distance around a circle." He circled his index finger around the fruit to demonstrate its meaning.

"I know this. But are you trying to tell me the earth is a ball, like that orange?"

Joseph stammered. "You, you do not know that, that the Earth is a ball?" He took a seat, frowning.

"This is not common knowledge in the Blue Nile," Israel interjected.

"And there have been times in the last three thousand years when many other places failed to recognize this basic fact. Until European sailors first crossed the Atlantic, some two thousand years after this well was dug, most people in that continent believed the world was flat."

Joseph frowned. "They did? I don't understand. How come if the Earth was known to be round long ago, people that came later did not know?"

Israel shrugged. "Knowledge is something not easily passed from generation to generation. It is work. Like going to this well to get water. Sometimes people find it easier to simply drink the water that comes down the river. After a while, they stop going to the well. In time, they forget where the well is altogether."

Joseph and Jasmine 2

Joseph spent the night above deck, staring at the stars and moon until sleep set in. Below deck Jasmine took shelter in a crawl space in the bow where she laid canvas sacks as a crude but comfortable bed. Cleopatra would join her most of the night before slipping away to wander the boat and explore its many niches. Joseph lay on the bare wood with only a jersey rolled into a pillow beneath his head for comfort.

One night Jasmine awoke to find her cat gone and began to search the ship frantically. Not finding her pet below deck, she went above and continued to search. She was consumed by the fear that Cleopatra had strayed overboard. She came across Joseph beside the cargo hold, fast asleep on his back and snoring like a human foghorn. She jostled him awake with her toe against his shoulder. "Wake up, Joseph," she commanded.

Hearing the alarm in her voice, Joseph leapt to his feet ready to meet the emergency of the moment. He looked wildly over the length of the boat expecting to see a fire or evidence of the boat taking on water. Jasmine stood beside him, stunned by his intensity and the closeness of his naked torso.

"Where is it?" he bellowed.

"I don't know. That's why I woke you up."

Joseph eyed her, perplexed. "Why did you wake me up?"

"Have you seen Cleopatra?" she pleaded.

"I was asleep. Of course I didn't see your cat." Joseph's voice was brittle with contempt in the manner he would chastise a man in his charge.

She was unaccustomed to such treatment and hovered near tears, already upset by the disappearance of her cat. "I can't find her anywhere. I think she is in the river." Her voice broke, and she cast her gaze downward to hide imminent tears.

He looked at her in her sullen state and felt it strange to see someone so openly exposed. His training and the culture he had spent his adulthood in forbade such displays of weakness. He gathered his jersey and dressed it loosely over his chest. "Don't be afraid. Animals know better than to leap to their deaths."

Jasmine looked up, drying her eyes with the back of her hand. "I am sorry to have woken you. But what if you are wrong?"

"I'm not. Relax. Go back to bed and your cat will come to you."

"I can't sleep. I am too afraid."

"You are worried, and this is a bad thing."

"I know it is bad," she snapped back.

He was bemused by the sharpness of her reply. "What I mean, Jasmine, is there are always things out of our hands, and we can only hope for the best. Getting upset won't help at all, so just imagine Cleopatra sneaking back into your bed with you while you sleep the way she has done a thousand times before."

Her eyes dried, and her brow relaxed. She looked up to him, embarrassed. "You are a nice man to care about a stupid girl and her cat." She leaned over and kissed him then turned and went below. In her bed, she fell asleep and was visited by Cleopatra before dawn.

Above, Joseph stared into the heavens and did not sleep at all.

Israel 3

Following this encounter Jasmine removed her veil without saying why. Joseph was assisting Israel with a repair of the bilge pump when the captain took the opportunity to speak in private. Joseph cranked the pump while Israel mended the seals that were in no small part responsible for keeping the small craft afloat.

"Jasmine has shed her veil," said the captain. Joseph only nodded, focused more on the task at hand. "Don't tell me you did not notice?"

"I noticed," he replied.

"You did notice. That's good. It is of concern to me when a man doesn't take notice of a pretty woman's face." Joseph continued to pump. "Are you aware that it is her people's custom to only show their face before trusted friends and family?"

"I gathered as much."

"It may seem a small matter, but it is not to go unnoticed."

"I suppose."

"If I were a man of your years, I would be more interested in the whole business. A woman's company is worth more than a boatload of glory."

Joseph looked up from his task and met the old man's puzzled stare. "I have learned to ignore such things."

"Why?"

"Because I am a foreigner and a centurion, so women are forbidden to me."

Israel frowned. "Forbidden?"

"Punishable as among the severest of transgressions. My duty is to keep people where they belong, not to go as I please."

"You make it sound noble, but to my thinking an oath of celibacy is an abomination, especially for a young man."

Joseph bit his lip and looked away, then returned to cranking the bilge pump.

Joseph and Jasmine 3

Later on the trip, a weather front passed by that brought rain. Joseph's attempt to fashion a tarp into a shelter left much to be desired. The wind billowed it in a manner that dowsed him in the face with water that had pooled in the recesses of the makeshift roof. He cursed when this happened, and his cursing pierced the patter of the rain as Jasmine rested below.

She called to him, "Joseph, what are you doing up there?"

His frustration boiled over. "I am sleeping."

"You snore in your sleep, but I have never heard you curse."

"Go back to bed. I am fine."

"I am not fine. I cannot sleep with the sound of a man cursing. Now please come down below deck."

"I am going to stay here where I can watch the stars and moon."

"You can't see the stars and moon tonight, Joseph! It is time to come out of the rain."

"No!"

Jasmine giggled lightly at the childlike sound of his answer, but thought better of teasing him while he was angry. "For my sake, please."

Below deck he fumbled in the darkness, tipping over barrels and tripping on rigging. This continued for a while before Jasmine again intervened, "There is room up here," she said motioning for him to join her in the berth. Joseph looked up to her with rainwater dripping from his hair, but otherwise frozen in place. "Don't make me ask twice," she said with finality.

Joseph removed his jersey and used it to sponge the water from his hair. He climbed up into the berth beside her and found room under her blanket. He slid his arm around the curve of her side and drew her close and kissed her. She pressed her palm against his chest and calmly said, "You have nice skin."

He looked into her eyes, brown within white set in their charcoal orbs and could not break his gaze. "You have nice skin, too." They undressed and joined carelessly together.

At the other end of the boat, Captain Israel awoke to the sound of something other than the wind and rain pelting sails and decking. Faintly he could discern the creaking of the boards of Jasmine's berth. He smiled and rolled over, falling again to sleep.

THE BOOK OF THE KHARTOUM

Izzi 1

Two months before the Great Passover

Izzi clutched the hair on his chin as he read a bill posted on a tree in the Khartoum Green. The hair of his face was a matted web of tangles more than it was a beard. At any given moment, particles from his previous meal could be found nested in this mass of snarled facial hair. He read the bill aloud, as his capacity for language did not extend to reading in silence. "Positions available for those who can leave Khartoum before Passover. Land and diamonds offered as compensation."

The Khartoum Green, while renowned for its natural beauty, was home to many indigents like Izzi and as such was considered a less than optimal place to post anything. The notion of leaving Khartoum before Passover had great appeal to a person without means who knew they stood a greater risk of selection come Passover's annual cull. Land and diamonds were the only things that could elevate a man of his station to a bearable existence. A man without land or diamonds wanted nothing more than to acquire them.

While it seemed too good to be true, there was some validity to it. The end of the bill mentioned a meeting in the Khartoum Grotto. This was not a place available to unsanctioned confidence men. If this business had access to the grotto, then it must have some legitimacy, and he felt compelled to attend. Besides, he had nothing to lose.

The captain of the *Terrier* strode to the rear of the altar of the Khartoum Grotto. From here he could be certain that all in attendance could see clearly the spectacle he was about to reveal. When the din of the crowd had relented to the man standing motionless before them, he drew the drawstrings of the fine leather pouch staged front and center on the altar. Nonchalantly, he spilled the contents of the purse for all to see. The act was met with gasps of disbelief, then exclamations of surprise, before returning to a pristine silence.

"Gentlemen," the lead agent spoke as he stepped to the front of the altar. "We have diamonds..." Peals of laughter echoed off the stone walls. "And we have work...Enough to make you wealthy and landed. For those of you prepared to sign and seal contracts tonight, we are prepared to advance a sum sufficient to buy the parcel of your choice from an elite downstream realtor. Join our effort tonight, and you will sail upstream tomorrow with your land titles and future secured."

Israel 4

Captain Israel climbed the steps and entered the office of the Khartoum harbormaster. "Channel Runner!" called a man behind a desk. He was gray but fit, and he wore his uniform with special attention to detail. Over the years, he had accumulated a host of badges that adorned his shirt.

"At your service, Mr. Harbormaster." The men smiled and shook hands warmly.

"I understand you had some guests on your way up from Aswan." He seated himself behind his desk and gestured towards a chair for Israel to sit in.

"Artemis, you know all."

"That's why they give me these badges. Can I get you a drink, Israel?"

Israel nodded and sat back in his chair. The harbormaster unlocked a drawer and pulled out a bottle of coffee liqueur. "You have come a long way. You deserve the best." Israel took the glass that had been poured. "Isn't it a blessing when a friend comes from afar?"

"It is a greater blessing to travel far and find a friend." The men clanked their glasses and drank a mouthful before putting them down.

"Aaah…good stuff, Artemis. Thank you kindly."

"Always a pleasure to please."

"So, you know of my passengers?"

"No, but I have heard a man and a woman left the *Pursuit of Happiness* upon arrival."

"Yes, Jasmine and Joseph. A good pair to have onboard for a long voyage."

"They are a couple?" His eyebrows rose high.

"Not at the moment. Both seemed to have better places to go than into each other's arms."

"Where might they be headed?"

"The girl wants a new life downstream. The man wants an old life upstream."

He leaned forward in his chair. "This man, he is destined for the interior?"

"He is destined for trouble, if you ask me." Israel tilted his head and sipped more of his drink.

His host refilled their glasses. "I see. Well, here is to trouble, a most worthy destiny." They clinked and gulped again.

"Aaah. Even sweeter than the first." Israel slouched in his chair while Artemis sat up straight.

"The girl is going the wrong way, if she means to be headed downstream."

"She needs to take care of some paperwork a Census official says she is missing. You know the drill in Aswan: Lay me or pay me."

Artemis looked to the ceiling briefly. "I see. It can be a hard world on those who are broke and maintain high virtues."

"Ohhh. Amen, and pour me another." His host obliged. "To being broke and having no virtue!"

The harbormaster laughed, but did not join in this third drink.

"What brings the man here?"

"The same thing that brought me here, his transfer."

"He is a centurion?" He sat back, lifting his eyebrows high.

"Aye. A centurion officer. Here to fight the good fight. Hitching a ride on a reserve vessel activated just for the purpose of taking him south."

Artemis bent over laughing. "You were activated? That means you are on active duty, now. If I knew that, Israel, I never would have broken out the booze."

"Artemis, I know for a fact that you were half drunk during the times you earned half those badges you're wearing today. And the other half you earned for good housekeeping." Artemis smiled but did not laugh. "You know all too well that a young soldier earns badges for being foolish, and an old soldier wears them for being vain."

"Yes, I confess. I love my badges, and you love your drink. So can we toast to them both?" A clink and a gulp later, both men began to slur their speech. "This young soldier, is he the foolish type?"

"I see badges in his future. He'll die trying, anyway."

"What is his rank?"

"Lieutenant, going on general." Israel nodded repeatedly, looking slightly glassy eyed.

"Brave men have ambitions. Sometimes a bad lieutenant makes for a good captain."

"Oh, he is brave enough to lead, I assure you. But he may be too brave to follow. A dangerous mix in a war zone."

"You should know, old friend. This Joseph sounds just like you."

"Maybe. Maybe this is why I wish he would take that girl's hand and let the rest of the world go to hell."

Izzi 2

The Great Green of Khartoum sloped up from the lagoon to the very steps of the courthouse. The effect of the building's posture overlooking the expanse of land and water in the midst of an otherwise crowded urban center was to convey the eminent purpose of the institution, defending the natural world. As they climbed the flower flanked pathways under the shade of blossoming cherry trees, they passed the Eternal Fountain.

The fountain was a memorial to martyred centurions lost in battles in the perennial conflict to salvage the Upper Nile. All pathways leading to the courthouse converged here, obligating entrants to observe the shrine to the Census. Joseph and Jasmine paid their quiet respects to the countless fallen guardians. And they were not alone. Scores of men were arranged in concentric arcs stretching halfway around the fountain.

Jasmine recognized one of these men as a native of her village. "Izzi!"

He turned quizzically, hesitant to break his stoic posture and expression. "Jasmine!" he exclaimed in unmuted surprise.

"What brings you to the courthouse?"

"Well, we are all gathered to receive our Oath of Indenture."

"You are becoming a centurion!"

"Yes, and I am shipping out this evening…" A chorus of shushing resonated from the men within earshot of the conversation. "But this must be kept in strictest confidence, of course."

"Of course, Izzi. Your secrets are safe with me."

"And with me," interrupted Joseph. He closed the distance between himself and the man with whom Jasmine was familiar. "My name is Joseph, and I am an officer in the Census," he said as he rolled up his sleeve to reveal the brand of a centurion officer.

"Sir, yes, sir," Izzi replied, standing straight. Those around him did likewise.

"Relax, recruits," Joseph chided. "Obviously this is your first day, and you have not learned that an officer out of uniform is not to be saluted. Now you know better."

The ranks relaxed, and laughter percolated through the formation.

"Can an officer out of uniform conduct the Oath of Indenture?" an anonymous voice asked from a distance.

Joseph paused. "I can do that, if truth be known," he returned for all to hear.

A mumbling ensued in the group of recruits. "Someone get the notary!" yelled another.

Izzi looked to Joseph. "Sir, we have been here since this morning waiting to be inducted, but an officer has not been found to perform the ritual. Would it be possible for you to do it in the presence of the Justice of the Peace?"

"I see. This sounds like a desperate situation. For you, that is." The reflexive dealmaker was laying the groundwork for future negotiations.

Within a few minutes, the Khartoum Justice of the Peace appeared at the fountain. "I understand you are an officer."

Joseph again revealed his brand, as was appropriate when being certified by a judge. "Skin doesn't lie."

"These men have been waiting all day, but we haven't been able to find an officer to perform the oath."

"That is odd. How could you have a formation without an officer?"

"They assembled here this morning to conduct civil business."

"Civil business? All of them?"

"Apparently it was imperative that they conduct land transactions. In order to consummate the contract, though, they must all be sworn into the Census."

"Well, I certainly would like to help, Your Honor. I do have one request, though."

"Yes. What is it? Never met a centurion willing to do something for nothing."

"Well, it is a small matter, I assure you. This lady beside me has to attain some documentation asserting her custody of her cat."

"Whatever on Earth for, I can't imagine. But no matter, I can place her first in line with the judge of probate, who can give her any document she needs."

"Excellent. Let's do it."

Joseph bowed his head, and the men followed suit. He closed his eyes, sighed deeply and spoke from memory:

"With God as my witness

I pledge to uphold the spirit of the Roman Census

and the letter of its laws,

to guard the statutes of the Nile Protocol,

and to obey the leadership appointed above me until my last breath is drawn.

So help me God, Amen."

The men echoed in chorus, "Amen."

With the oath completed, Joseph put the men at ease. "You are centurions. You are on the front lines in the fight. You are on call to go in harm's way. As such, I would highly recommend that you put your affairs in order in the event of your untimely demise. It is the opinion of this Census officer that men who lose their lives should not lose their estates as well. While you are protecting the world, take care to protect your dependents.

"Some of you may think yourselves invincible. This fountain is testament to the fact that you are not. Some of you may believe there is no one to leave your estate to. I am sure that all of you know one person who you feel is more deserving of your life's work than the Treasurer of the Roman Census."

A din arose in the ranks as the men queried each other as who their benefactor would be. All were more accustomed to the destitution of their past than the role of landed gentry in their future. Few could say readily to whom they could assign an inheritance.

The man next to Izzi turned to him and asked, "Izzi, who is the love of your life?"

Quiet swelled in his immediate vicinity. Meanwhile, Joseph had walked to the rear of the formation and reunited with Jasmine. Before they headed into the courthouse, she paid her respects to him. "It has been good to see a face from home. Take care, Izzi."

"Jasmine, can I ask you for a favor?"

"What can I do?"

"You are headed to the judge of probate?"

"Yes."

"We will not have time to file our wills before shipping out. Could you do me the favor of filing my simple will?"

"I would be happy to, Izzi."

He produced a small document from his wallet. "Jasmine, since I left our homeland, I have been alone in the world. Would you do me the honor of serving as my heiress? It would please me to see a woman from my village assume my estate."

"Izzi, I am the one who is honored."

He filled out the document and handed it to her, bowing his head.

Ever the eavesdropper, Joseph stepped to the front, fully aware of the transaction taking place between her and Izzi. "Wait a minute, soldier," he interrupted. "This document needs to be witnessed by an officer." Izzi looked from Joseph to Jasmine with total confusion. Joseph took the card in hand, turned it over, and wrote his signature. "No charge."

Jasmine and Izzi broke into smiles and thanked him for his kind favor. Then, spontaneously, almost the entire unit besieged Jasmine and Joseph requesting the same treatment their comrade had just received. Within a few minutes, she had been assigned the beneficiary to the lands promised to the fateful troops shipping out for the upper reaches of the Blue Nile.

Joseph 5

Joseph returned to the military docks to collect his seabag and bid farewell to Captain Israel. At the entrance to the dock, he was surprised to encounter armed guards regulating pedestrian traffic through the gate.

"Sir, the docks are secured. Please state your business."

Joseph halted. "I am an officer of the Census aboard the *Pursuit of Happiness.*"

The guard unrolled a scroll in the guard shack that contained the ship's manifest. "Sir, please approach and try not to blink." Joseph approached and met the heavy stare of the guard. "Your name?" the guard asked without the slightest change of expression.

With the steely gaze upon him, the unflinching face of the guard sent a twinge of fear down the spine of Joseph. He saw a grave expression uncommon among soldiers with menial duties. This was a man who surely could take another's life if so instructed. Peering into the remorseless stare of this fellow centurion, he felt as though he was a prisoner of a hostile army, no matter that the men shared the same uniform. "I am Joseph."

After a short pause, the guard broke his silence. "Sir, please sign the log."

Joseph was relieved that his silent interrogation was over. "I am new to Khartoum. Not that vigilance is not a virtue, but do you always stop officers returning to their ship?"

"Tonight we have special orders." The guard's words cut into those of Joseph and ended with iron finality.

This manner of speaking to an officer occurred to Joseph as peculiar for a common guard. "So I guess that makes tonight a special night."

"Every night is a special night for a centurion," the guard replied with obvious sarcasm. Joseph passed through the gate under the still scrutinizing watch of the vigilant guard.

The water between the *Terrier* and the *Pursuit of Happiness* was undisturbed by wake or wind, a rare state for the busy military port. Both vessels shared the lagoon, but whereas the *Terrier* was at one end of the docks where cranes were poised to load and unload heavy cargo, the *Pursuit of Happiness*, already fully loaded with the stores Captain Israel would require for his lonely descent down the river, occupied the far end of the docks. From this distance, a person on one boat was unrecognizable by the unaided eye of a person on the other. However, at this distance semaphores were still clearly legible, enabling a lengthy dialogue of code between Captain Israel and the captain of the *Terrier*. The men waved their flags back and forth, piercing the boredom of the emptied docks with humor, gossip, and boastful tales of lifetime sailors.

"Joseph," the captain spoke, as soon as Joseph had cleared the gangplank onto the ship's deck, "there is a bottle of scotch in your seabag."

"You are too kind. To what do I owe such generosity?" Joseph's words lilted with a careless humor.

The captain was straightforward with his communication. Almost any other time he might have reciprocated Joseph's playful jests with comeback after comeback. In fact, the men had traded barbs for almost the entire time of their journey. But on this evening he waxed serious.

"It is for you, but not for your consumption."

Joseph considered the riddle. "Is it for the harbormaster?"

"Yes. See to it that he drinks more of it than you."

The *Pursuit of Happiness* shoved off into the setting sun, the silhouette of the captain at the helm passing into the dusk, vanishing from sight. Joseph imagined his safe descent down the Nile and pondered the loss of the man's company. Time on the small boat had forged an intimacy between its cohabitants, despite Joseph's inclinations towards privacy. Probably the lack of close ties to his peers in Aswan acted to magnify the bond formed between Joseph and Jasmine and Israel on their passage. His thoughts turned to memories of his fellow crew members. For a man with no family, his friends were his relatives. He wished the boat ride could last forever, carrying all three around the world in an unending voyage. Standing on the dock, watching Captain Israel disappear from view, he wondered if Jasmine would miss old Israel as much as he would.

She was still in Khartoum, but he discounted the likelihood that they might meet again in such a big city when they lead such different lives. Would she miss him as much as he missed her? He wondered if the adventures that lay ahead for him would be full compensation for the loss of the company of such a fine woman.

Jasmine 4

Bureaucratic Relics

The position of City Clerk was a relic of the system of patronage that was prevalent prior to the rise of the judges. According to current teaching, this ephemeral administrative function was preserved out of respect for its historic role as a rubber stamp for all the legal proceedings that comprised the Revolution of Judges.

Many would argue that it was the lack of integrity of clerks that led them to be co-opted by the judges, betraying the old republic in exchange for the preservation of their plum positions. In any event, the position of local clerk and probate judge remained elected, inefficient, and as corrupt as ever. They also provided a semblance of democracy in a system that otherwise was devoid of popular influence, satisfying the timeless need of the masses for a sense of control, no matter how superficial and rudimentary were the powers of these positions.

—*Book of History*

Jasmine walked into the office of the clerk with an official escort, one of the few ways a person could be assured prompt service. The elderly Jacob presented himself with hands intertwined and head bowed. "Ma'am, I am at your service." The escort left Jasmine's side without a word spoken.

"Thank you, sir. I understand you have been willing to stay beyond your normal hours for my benefit."

"I understand an officer of the Census was willing to perform duty while on leave for our sake. Quite a fair exchange in my book." The man's wrinkles relaxed into a smile. "You should marry a man as shrewd as this gentleman. He would be a good provider!"

She laughed at the clerk's blunt delivery and blushed at the suggestion of marriage to Joseph. She felt at ease knowing this official was not expecting any further compensation. "I have several papers I need to file." She produced a stack from her saddlebag. "Can you register these?"

Jacob perused the documents, all forms designating her as the beneficiary of the estates of the newly sworn-in centurions. "I will register these with the Office of Probate without delay."

She then passed Jacob a small scroll distinct from the others. Jacob opened the slender scroll and read the heading aloud, "'Declaration of Dependency.' How old is your dependent?"

"I am not sure. She was no longer a kitten when I found her."

Jacob looked at her with a wry smile. "This is for your cat? What in the world for?"

Her face reddened. "It is a requirement of the immigration office in Aswan."

"This is ridiculous. There is no such requirement. And the use of this document for a pet is ludicrous. Why should immigration want this?"

Her eyes began to tear as she remembered her encounter with Martin.

"What the immigration officer wants is more than proper documentation. This red tape is his way of having revenge on me for refusing him."

Jacob offered her a tissue. "Ma'am, I can certify any document you present me, but I am afraid this Declaration of Dependency for your cat will not satisfy this official."

"But then, what will?"

Jacob stopped to think. He certainly did not want to fail the centurion who had referred her to him. He was obligated to find a solution.

"There is one document that no immigration officer will dare stymie: a marriage certificate of a centurion."

She tilted her head disapprovingly. "Sir, please be serious. There must be some way for me to immigrate. It is my right, is it not?"

"It is. But I am in Khartoum, and you wish to exit, not enter the bounds of my authority. There are few remedies available to me that will prevail over a rogue outpost of the Census."

From the steps of the City Hall, she looked out over the Eternal Fountain and the grounds leading down to the lagoon. These grounds, which first impressed her as majestic displays of the essential providence of the modern order, now failed to move her with the same spiritual moment. She clumsily fumbled inside her saddlebag, finally finding her rosary string. *It is a small sacrifice to make the world green again*, she prayed with tears welling up in her eyes. Her sacrifice seemed larger all the time. To her eyes, the grounds of Khartoum looked devoid of life, like a building or a road. She saw the vegetation, carefully placed and sculpted, as a vulgar act of humanity instead of an indelible mark of the Creator.

She longed for the unbridled wilderness of the Upper Nile. Feeling lost in the great city, she sought out the only part with which she was familiar. She strode quickly in hopes of reaching the offices of the University of Khartoum before all occupants had vacated for the night. Here she could find her geology professor from her brief tenure of study.

The sun was setting over the lagoon, and from her vantage, she could see the outline of a vessel heading away towards the Nile. She recognized this as the form of the *Pursuit of Happiness*. Although she was pressed for time, she paused solemnly to ponder the departure of the good Captain Israel. This man had rescued her from the travails of Aswan. And he did so out of the simple desire to help an innocent soul. *Who will deliver me from Khartoum?* she wondered, not at all certain that she would meet a person as generous as the captain in this city of strangers.

Despite its status as an administrative and military capitol, Khartoum's lone campus of higher learning was a small affair lacking any delusions of grandeur or even a hint of prestige. The city's intelligentsias were the graduates of prestigious downstream universities and they looked down on the modest local college with contempt and ridicule. Focused on supporting Khartoum's government agencies with clerical staff, the University of Khartoum's motto was "*Gateway to Governance.*" Derisive versions of this official phrase included "*Gateway to Subservience,*" as well as many others.

She had attended UK and quickly exhausted all of the meager course offerings that were even closely related to the subject of geology. There was no Earth science department at UK, only one professor, Alfonso Baruch, whose specialty was geology. His existence in the curriculum was an oddity, providing a course of study inconsequential to the core mission of vocational preparation.

When she arrived at KU this evening, Baruch was playing a game of solitaire, as he usually did during his assigned office hours. He dutifully made himself available to his students, but they seldom took advantage of this time to seek individualized help. Most were taking his course with little interest other than to fulfill the one-course science requirement.

As a student, she had been eager to learn everything she could about geology and was one of those exceptional students who came to Baruch outside of his lecture. When she knocked on his open door, he greeted her heartily. "Jasmine! Welcome! Please come in! What can I do for you?" Dr. Baruch was typically over-enthusiastic about everything, so this boisterous welcome was nothing out of the ordinary.

"I am not sure you can do anything for me, Alfonso," she replied. All students who knew the man for more than one conversation felt entirely comfortable speaking to him on a first-name basis. And so she recounted her unfortunate tale of her attempts to emigrate below Aswan in hopes of attending a top-notch downstream university.

With both hands pushed deep into his pants pockets, Alfonso asked, "Jasmine, I must ask, what is it you hope to achieve by studying at a downstream university?"

"I want to be a geologist."

"And then what will you do?"

She paused, stunned temporarily with the directness with which this scientist was laying plain her secret plans. Until now she had guarded her dreams from disclosure, especially from her friends and acquaintances out of fear that she would lose face should she fall short of her goals.

Sensing her unease, the professor did not wait longer for her answer. "If you know where you are headed, this is more important than where you have been. We spend our lives going from alpha to omega. Today you are at alpha, and you believe a degree in geology is beta. But if you are sure of what your omega is, perhaps then I can help you to skip a few letters."

His kindness allowed her to dismiss the fear of embarrassment inhibiting her from divulging her most privately held secret. In a calm, sturdy voice, she declared her intimate intentions. "I want to return to my homeland, in the wilderness of the Blue Nile."

The professor digested her statement, chin down in the web of his thumb, his arms folded across his chest. After a brief stare into infinity, he broke the impenetrable silence that followed her confession. "What I can suggest is seeking an university referral to the Geologic Survey. The GS posts certain openings with UK, and I have seen some openings posted and reposted without being filled. Most are only temporary assignments that don't draw any applicants. Even though you may be unqualified for a position in the survey, beggars can't be choosers."

Jasmine smiled, and color filled her cheeks. "That would be wonderful! Are you certain?"

He spread his arms wide and drew a deep breath before he spoke. "Of course, my dear. It will happen. I will make it happen. And when you get this post, I will be as happy as you."

Jasmine rushed to him and embraced him under his open arms. He could only laugh and embrace her back.

She broke away and was readying to leave when she thought of something more. "I have another favor to ask."

He seated himself and turned his palms upward. "How can I help?"

"It is a question of geology."

"You will not stump me, I hope."

"South of Aswan, I was shown a well. I was told that the sun could shine down to the bottom of this well, but only on the first day of summer."

Baruch's face straightened. "This well was on the Tropic of Cancer."

Jasmine's eyes widened. "Yes. I was told this. Is it true that north of here light never reaches the bottom of a well?"

Baruch nodded. "This is the truth."

"Is it also true that the reason this is so has something to…with the world being a ball?"

Baruch stared at a point slightly to the right of Jasmine. After a few moments, he muttered softly, "It is not my place to say."

The color drained from Jasmine's face. "It is the truth. And you know it. Why do you say it is not for you to say?"

Baruch sat and met her glaring eyes. "If I say, you must not share this knowledge with anyone."

"Why?"

"Why? Because it is forbidden! My predecessor taught of such things, and he was stripped of his doctorate."

"For teaching the truth?"

"For cultivating unrest in the hearts and minds of our students. This is not a matter the Census takes lightly."

Jasmine seated herself across the room from Baruch. "You can trust me, Professor. But, please, tell me more about the shape of the world."

Baruch lit a candle and rolled up a piece of paper into a narrow tunnel. He picked up a coconut and held the rolled up paper between the coconut and the candle. Light from the candle created a disk on the coconut, and he rotated the coconut and the paper in tandem about the flame. "The world is the shape of a ball, like the sun and the moon. And just as the moon travels around the earth, the earth travels around the sun. Because the earth does not face the sun directly, the direct rays of the sun strike the earth at a different place each day. On the first day of summer, they hit on the Tropic of Cancer." He pointed to a place on the top half of the coconut. "From then, until the first of winter, the direct rays occur further and further to the south. After the first of winter, they occur further and further to the north, until summer begins again with them shining on the Tropic of Cancer."

Having received her lesson, Jasmine stood and bowed. "Thank you, Baruch."

He mopped sweat from his brow with his sleeve but did not reply. She turned to leave, and had taken a step toward the door when she looked back and asked, "Why is it wrong for you to teach such things?"

He shook his head sideways and sank his hands deep into his pant pockets. "It is not for me to know."

Joseph 6

Joseph climbed the stairs to the harbormaster's office, passing into darkness at the entrance. He knocked twice and waited. "Enter," the harbormaster called from his seat behind his desk.

Joseph entered and stood at attention before his host. "I am Joseph, and I was told you wished to see me."

The harbormaster stood. "My name is Artemis. Thank you for accepting my invitation." He gestured towards a seat before seating himself. "Your captain mentioned you are a promising centurion."

"He did? Well, that was generous of him."

"He is a generous man, Israel. You are fortunate to have such a captain."

"Actually, he is no longer my captain, but he is, indeed, a generous man." He pulled from his seabag the bottle Israel had given him. "This is for you."

Artemis received the bottle and opened it at once. "May I pour you a drink?"

"Well, I am on leave…"

Artemis raised his glass and gave a toast, "To Captain Israel."

Joseph took his glass and raised it. "Long may he sail." The men clinked glasses and drank, then set their glasses back down. "Israel is a curiosity. He is the most learned sailor I have ever met."

"Yes, well, he used to be a professor here in Khartoum." His words were a notch below sober diction.

"Really? He never mentioned this."

"His career was cut short. He probably would prefer to forget this part of his life. Most of us do have a portion of our lives that we would rather not remember."

"Sir, I wish to toast to painful memories long forgotten." The men clinked and drank. Joseph carefully sipped while Artemis took a whole gulp.

Artemis leaned on his desk. "You are probably curious about why I asked for you."

"I am."

"But you do well to conceal it. This is good. A centurion needs to be patient when it comes to learning the reasoning of his superiors."

"I have no cause to doubt my leaders."

"Doubt of one's leaders is a disease for a soldier. A soldier must act without thinking, without knowing why. And the same must be true of those who serve below you." Joseph nodded in affirmation. "If you wish others to follow you, you must, in turn, follow others."

"This seems perfectly logical."

"It is perfectly logical. And a leader must exercise a keen sense of logic. But logic is not enough. Israel is one of the most logical men I know, but would you follow him into battle?"

Joseph considered the question. After a brief time, he answered, "I suppose not."

"And why not?" Artemis's brows raised high.

"It is hard for me to say…only a feeling I have about him…"

"You see! No logical reason at all, and yet you have this 'feeling'. These 'feelings' are our beliefs, and they are not always logical. When a commander orders a man to go into harm's way, both men must ultimately believe in the cause they serve."

Joseph extended his arm, holding his half-empty glass. "To the cause we serve."

Artemis, finding his glass empty, hurriedly refilled it before raising it and meeting the glass of his guest. As he drank, some of the liquid escaped, falling to the desk blotter below. "Do you know why Israel no longer teaches at our university?"

"I did not know the man ever taught before I came through this door, but may I venture a guess?"

"Surely. If you know the man, you can make a good guess."

"Well, I imagine he had some difficulty with his superiors."

"Of course. The Roman Census maintains the right to restrict the curriculum of any place of higher learning. Do you know why?" Joseph shook his head. "Because knowledge is a tree that grows without bound. People deserve to be taught well, we all agree, so they can serve our holy mission to the best of their skills and abilities. No one should be limited in this regard." Joseph nodded. "But beyond this, people who pursue knowledge for knowledge's sake inevitably run afoul."

Joseph frowned. "How is this so?"

"A tree in the orchard needs limbs for fruit to grow. But limbs without fruit only take away from those that do. Too much knowledge is a bad thing."

Joseph sat back and met the stare of the man speaking to him. "I suppose an argument could be made that knowledge of weaponry caused the demise of the ancient world."

"Exactly! This is what Israel failed to see. He didn't see the harm of his teachings, and he lost faith in the way of our world."

Joseph put his glass down empty. "I know the truth of a tree by the fruit it bears. I see the land improve, the Earth heal, and the people at peace. This is enough for me to believe in the goodness of what we do."

"Then I have a job for you."

"Yes?"

"I want you to go with the *Terrier* to the frontier."

Joseph's brow crinkled slightly. "And do what?"

Artemis smiled and shrugged his shoulders. "To defend the faith."

Joseph folded his arms. "That isn't a lot to go on."

Artemis eased back in his chair. "Like I said, a centurion has to believe in his leaders."

"In this case, that would mean you. Can you tell me why you are someone I should believe in?"

The harbormaster pointed to his chest. "You see these badges?" Joseph nodded. "You don't get these for doing a good job checking cargo manifests. I have gone in harm's way to uphold our oath to the Nile. I have endured hardships and loss but never lost faith.

"Over the years, I have seen the toll of the Passover take people from me. I know that sometimes innocent people must die and the guilty go free. Otherwise, there would be no order. And then, all would be lost. The population would grow and consume all of nature's gifts, leaving behind ruined land and foul water.

"Both my wife and daughter were lost in the same Passover. I grieve them still, of course. But I bear no malice to the Protocol that asks us to sacrifice all so that all is not lost. It is enough for me that only a few who are good perish, while the bad are far more likely to pay for their sins.

"Even if I have been unlucky, I am not ungrateful. The world today requires us to make sacrifices. If I had the chance and were young again, I would gladly do the job myself. I am not asking of you anything more than what I would be willing to risk myself."

Joseph's eyes blinked, but not before a tear could escape. "What must I do?"

Artemis opened his desk drawer and removed a scroll bound with a black ribbon. "You are to lead a company of raw recruits on a patrol of the Ethiopian border. Along the way, you will be assigned other tasks."

Joseph came to the position of attention. "I accept this charge without condition."

"Good, good. Take this scroll to the captain of the *Terrier*. You and your men ship out this evening."

Joseph and saluted. "I will comply."

Artemis returned the salute. "God speed, Captain." Joseph did not respond, but his look betrayed his confusion. "This post comes with a promotion. Congratulations."

Jasmine 5

At the end of a hallway in Khartoum University's main administration building, a door without any markings opened to a stairway that led half a flight down to another door, also with no markings of any kind. Jasmine walked into the office of the university liaison to the Geological Survey of the Roman Census without knocking. A clean-shaven man in casual dress greeted her, "You must be Jasmine?"

"Yes, I am."

"Did you have any trouble finding the place?"

"None at all. Your directions were perfectly sound."

"I'm glad to hear that. A person who can't find this office has no business surveying the wilderness."

Jasmine did not respond at first, but instead searched the man's face for traces of humor. Finding none, she asked, "Does that mean I have the job?"

At this the man did smile. "As a matter of fact, it does." He walked over to a wall where a map of the Blue Nile was drawn. He pointed to a dot close to a dashed line demarking the boundary of the Nile Watershed. "You'll be working here, if that is acceptable?"

She glanced at the map on the wall briefly before answering, "That is fine. Can you tell me what the job entails?"

The man shrugged his shoulders and replied without much humor, "It entails going to this point on the map, doing what you are assigned, and not asking too many more questions. Is that still fine with you?" Jasmine nodded in the affirmative without any hesitation. "Good! Then I can sign you up and ship you out."

"Thank you, sir. You can't know how much it means to me to find work in my field."

The liaison handed her a form. "It is my pleasure. Please fill this out and you will be on your way."

Joseph 7

The *Terrie*r was barely visible in its berth in the time between sunset and moonrise. A lone lantern illuminated the gangplank. Joseph stood on the dock and noted that the gangplank slanted down from the dock. The waterline was above the last of the ascending numerals painted on the bow, obscuring the depth of the keel from plain view. Again, he wondered what might be onboard the vessel to make it sink so low.

He shared the dock with a huddle of men, the same men he had sworn into the Roman Census earlier in the day. Their incessant conversations created a palpable din. He called to them, "Fall in." They became silent, but did not organize the way a commander would expect his troops to do when ordered to formation.

Onboard the *Terrier*, its captain came above deck and peered out over the spectacle of a centurion officer staring at his men, giving an order, and the men merely staring back without moving. He removed his cap and scratched his bald scalp, smiling. "Centurion, are you sure these are your men?"

Joseph, still staring at the silent huddle, remained with his back to the *Terrie*r and its captain. He recognized in the group the old friend of Jasmine. "Izzi!" he called to him. Izzi raised an open palm to Joseph in the manner typical of greeting for a native of the Upper Nile. "Put your hands at your side when being addressed by your superior." Izzi complied immediately. "Now, stand there," Joseph ordered, pointing to a place five strides away and to his left. Izzi moved to this spot and stood with his palms to his side. Joseph pointed to a dozen of the men in front of him, "You soldiers, stand in a ring beside Izzi." The men stepped forward and took up positions in a rough semicircle around their commander. "The rest of you make more rings around this first rank, and do so without talking." The others shuffled into three more rings, all concentric about Joseph. "I am Captain Joseph. I am your commanding officer, and this is the general idea of what I expect to see happen when you are given the order to 'fall in'."

Joseph turned away from his formation of men towards the *Terrier* and its captain onboard. He put his palms at his side before raising his right hand to his brow. "Sir, Task Force Alpha requests permission to come aboard."

The captain replaced his cap and returned the salute. "First, I would like to address these men before they come on my ship." Joseph nodded his consent. The captain surveyed the group before him on the dock before speaking. "Your commander is your commander, wherever you go. But on this ship I am the only captain you will know, so it is the policy of the *Terrier* that you not address your commander by the rank of captain while onboard." Joseph and his men stood below, not moving, not speaking, and listening to his every word.

"Another policy of the *Terrier* is that you are all required to wash every day. After all, there are a lot of you and only one ship, so there is little room for us all but plenty of water in the river. It is a long trip, so please do your comrades a favor and spare us of your stench."

The men found amusement in these orders, and laughter rippled through their ranks. Joseph looked over his right shoulder and bellowed, "At ease!" He turned back to the captain and raised his hand again in a salute. "Task Force Alpha will comply."

The captain met Joseph's salute and held it while he spoke, "Request to come aboard granted." He finished his salute and went back below deck. Joseph finished his salute to the absent captain, then turned to his men and ordered them down the gangplank in an orderly fashion.

Lansing 1

Judge Lansing traced the furrows of his brow lightly with both of his index fingers. A lifetime of responsibilities had edged these crevices deep into his face so that an expression of concern persisted even in the absence of any serious matter. In his gaze at the moment was a stack of papers bound together by twine like a bale of hay. He looked up at the city clerk before him and asked, "What is this?"

"Today's papers for you to process, Your Honor."

"I realize that. What I don't understand is how this much work gets laid on my desk in a single day. Can you recall a stack like this, bound in twine, outside of post-Passover settlements?"

"No, I cannot."

"Then how did this get here?"

"Well, this morning a lady submitted them on behalf of a company of new Census recruits. These are their wills declaring her as the beneficiary of their estates."

The judge untied the twine holding together the stack of wills. He lifted up the first set of papers that together comprised the estate of one man. He leafed through the papers and then stopped suddenly. "This recruit's estate includes land in the delta!" He grabbed the next set of papers while the clerk stood by. "So does this man. Is this case common in this company of recruits?"

"It is, Your Honor. Every recruit in the company is a landowner. At least…" The clerk paused and then looked down without continuing.

"Speak your mind, you are not on the record."

The clerk looked the judge in the eye. "At least on paper they are landowners."

"And do you have any reason to doubt the legitimacy of the titles before me?"

"That is for the probate judge to decide, Your Honor."

The judge leaned over the papers before him. "Before I do, you are going to provide me a list of the former title holders of these properties going back thirty years. Understood?"

"Yes, Your Honor."

The judge reassembled the stack of papers and retied the twine about them. The clerk approached the bench and carried away the stack of wills and titles.

The Book of the Blue Nile

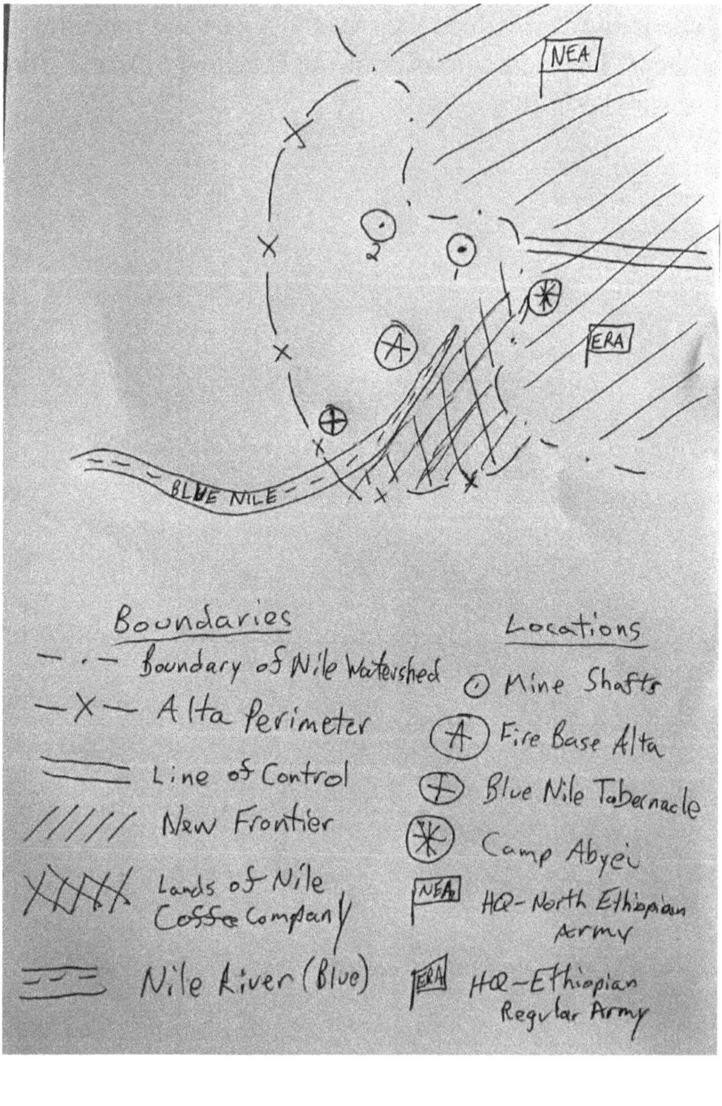

Joseph 8

Once underway, Joseph paid a visit to the ship's captain. It was obvious that the man had freshly oiled his scalp by the way the light of the lantern reflected off his crown. Joseph extended his left hand holding a scroll tied with black ribbon. "Sir, this is from the Khartoum harbormaster."

The captain of the ship took the scroll. "Take a seat, Captain."

Joseph cocked his head slightly. "I thought you were the only captain onboard?"

"No, I am the only one who may be called 'captain' to avoid confusion. Of course, I can call you 'captain' because I can tell the difference between us." He unrolled the scroll and read its contents, looking up after finishing. "What did the harbormaster tell you about your mission?"

"Very little."

"Very little? Well, it is his nature to be discreet. This scroll instructs me to confer to you a most privileged status within a particularly sensitive operation."

"Operation?"

"You are going to take a brief detour before reporting to Fire Base Alta. Cargo will be unloaded from the *Terrier* and taken to a location to be determined later. After this is accomplished, you will lead your men on a routine patrol of the Ethiopian border.

"As is usual, a bounty will be paid to your men in diamonds for the scrotum of every trespasser killed or captured. However, you are specifically ordered not to take any prisoners while on patrol. Instead, prisoners captured will be put to death and hung in a manner that will make plain the consequences of incursions across the boundary of the Nile Watershed." The captain of the *Terrier* passed Joseph a map of the territory he was to patrol.

Joseph made no response at first. Although the rumor of the diamond bounty was known to him, he was nevertheless surprised to hear the vague, almost mythical concept expressed as his formal orders. After he looked down at the map, lost in meditation and analysis, he looked up at the captain and asked, "I notice on this map that there are four quadrants, one of which I am to patrol. What are these other pieces of the puzzle?"

"You will patrol the northwest portion on this map. To the east across the mountains is rebel-held northern Ethiopia. South of there is loyalist Ethiopia, and south of your quadrant within the Nile watershed are the lands of the Nile Coffee Company."

"How likely are we to come across vagrants on this patrol?"

"Extremely likely. There is an incessant flow of coffee smuggled through this area."

"It would seem the Census is currently patrolling only the border with the rebels. Who is watching the frontier to prevent smuggling from loyal Ethiopia into Egypt?"

The captain shrugged his shoulders. "No one."

"Why is that?"

"Why is not your concern. The Census has no interest in coming between loyal Ethiopia and the Nile Coffee Company. Your task is to stop smugglers from passing into Egypt from northern Ethiopia."

Joseph returned to the map and explored it for more details. "Our encampment is far away from the trails we are to patrol. Is there a reason for this?"

"You mean Fire Base Alta?"

"Yes."

The captain intertwined his fingers and leaned forward. "You must return to Fire Base Alta to reinforce our position there."

"Yes, well, if we are to intercept smugglers by patrolling the border, doesn't it make more sense to have a strong position closer to the border?"

"You ask a lot of questions for a soldier." The captain met his eye with a wry smile.

"As an officer, I hope to improve the chances for a successful mission, even if this means reviewing the merits of our current operations."

"A good trait in any officer, but not in this case."

"Why?"

"There is that word again. I suppose you are entitled to know why your men will need to make camp a good distance from the border they are to patrol. In fact, the Khartoum Harbormaster has authorized me to brief you on the Phoenix Initiative if such information will serve to bolster your confidence in your orders. Obviously you have some doubts about the suitability of your orders to your mission.

"You are quite correct about the location of Fire Base Alta. It is most inconvenient as a base for border patrols. The reason you are being ordered to make camp there is to protect the ongoing operations of the Phoenix Initiative."

"Phoenix?"

"Yes, the city that sprung from the desert. A true story from the ancient world."

"True story?"

"Yes. There was a city named Phoenix that prospered in the midst of a barren landscape. Water was routed there from a river many horizons away by man-made aqueducts. Today we are implementing a similar scheme in the headwaters of the Blue Nile. Our goal is to divert the waters bound for the Nile into man-made aquifers deep below the surface. These subterranean rivers will carry much-needed water into the arable lands of northern Ethiopia."

"We are routing water of the Nile into northern Ethiopia? Why does Rome help the rebels with one hand and fight it with another?"

"The intent has never been to help the rebels in any way, shape, or form. In fact, when the Phoenix Initiative began forty years ago, there were no rebels. But that changed when the waters started to percolate in previously arid land. The Ethiopian government had trouble controlling events in these parts. So the aid of the Roman Census was enlisted to protect the new waters from being looted by the rebels.

"After twenty years of fighting them on their own turf, a border was drawn and a modus vivendi agreed to."

"Modus vivendi? I am not sure what this means."

"A cold truce. We don't recognize their claims of sovereignty, but we don't muster forces and perennially march them to their deaths to contest their claims, either."

"I see. So we have accepted defeat? I don't understand."

"No, not at all. We simply hope to achieve by embargo what we could not by conquest. If we can keep northern Ethiopia coffee from reaching Egyptian markets, then the land won't be worth it to them to hold. That is our strategy."

Joseph pondered the briefing he had just received. Then he shook his head, betraying a sense of confusion. "This still doesn't tell me why Fire Base Alta is so far from the patrols."

"If Fire Base Alta falls, reinforcements will have to march even further to reach the border, perhaps from Khartoum. You see, the creation of these aquifers, if not done carefully, could divert enough water from the Blue Nile to make it impossible to navigate by ship."

"The means to do this exists at Fire Base Alta?"

"Yes, in fact it does."

"How can this be?"

"This is where the engineers of the Phoenix Initiative are quartered. If they were to be captured, then the means to drain the Blue Nile into Ethiopia would be in the hands of the rebels." The captain unlaced his fingers and grabbed the armrests of his chair. "Need I explain the absolute sensitivity of the information that I have just provided you?"

Joseph shook his head from side to side. "No, sir. The gravity of this matter is self-evident."

"Then that is all, Captain. And, Joseph, for god's sake don't tell me you talk in your sleep."

Joseph grinned and shook his captain's hand before leaving.

Joseph and Jasmine 4

Jasmine and Joseph might never have met again after going their separate ways in Khartoum. But as is so often the case, these kindred souls shared similarities in their inclinations that overcame the many random movements of life that cause humanity at all times to be a cauldron of strangers.

It was their passion for the wide-open spaces that took them from the throng of Khartoum to the upper reaches of the Blue Nile. Joseph was commissioned to lead into battle the same ragtag army of desperados he had sworn into the Census in Khartoum. Jasmine was assigned to an engineering company that surveyed the nooks and crannies of the legendary "Valley of the Fallen," unknowingly in support of the covert Phoenix Initiative.

Both were billeted in the unassuming Fire Base Alta. Fortified against any imaginable attack, its structures lacked décor and blandly matched its surroundings in a reflexive attempt at camouflage, despite the fact that all within a week's walk of the place knew its exact location. It was the center of the grim Alta Perimeter, which extended to the northern Ethiopian frontier.

The Alta Firebase was a small community, and yet within it were several cliques that were oriented around separate duties, such as engineering and soldiering. These two camps performed their tasks apart, and seldom would individuals from one side have contact with the other.

This organization was designed to compartmentalize people with knowledge of state secrets in a way that would preempt the flow of information that is inevitable when people achieve intimacy.

A random act brought them out of their respective cocoons and into contact under a starlit night in the wilderness. Jasmine, in haste one evening while exiting her tent, failed to secure the tent flap before Cleopatra escaped into the darkness. It was her way to keep her pet enclosed in the confines of her tent when unleashed, as she worried of losing her longtime companion. Given half a chance, Cleopatra escaped to freedom at the first opportunity.

Chasing frantically, she drove the animal further away until the blackness of Cleopatra's fur could not be distinguished from the darkness of the night. So she went through the camp calling plaintively for her cat to return. This pathetic parade went on for some time, all the while she called out in vain.

From the days on the *Pursuit of Happiness,* Cleopatra had acquired the taste for military rations as fed her by Joseph on their ascent up the Nile. Not surprisingly, then, Cleopatra made a beeline for the centurion's mess hall. Here an incredulous Joseph, who had just sat down for a late dinner, recognized the cat. After allowing her to finish a snack plucked from his plate, much to the amusement of the centurions in attendance, he collected the cat in his arms and headed from the hall.

With desperation setting in, she continued her search, but in muted tones. The specter of life in this faraway place without a companion loomed large, as did the knowledge that a small domesticated cat was unlikely to survive in such a wild country. While her calls might never have brought on the willing return of a feline enjoying freedom and its favorite form of food, it did allow Joseph to locate her in the compound separating the engineers' portion of the base from that of the soldiers.

"Jasmine, is that you?"

"Joseph? What are you doing here?"

"Well, I…"

"Have you seen Cleopatra?"

At this Joseph opened his coat and exposed the purring Cleopatra, still feasting on a sliver of beef jerky within his uniform.

She rushed to recover her lost pet, reaching into Joseph's garment. Joseph put his arms around her, enclosing Cleopatra between them. She turned away from him as her face went pale. Still clutching the cat, she bent over and began to wretch. The vomit landed close to his boots, and he stepped back from her as she convulsed before him. After finishing she gave a sheepish look. "I am sorry about that."

Concern etched furrows into his brow. He kept his distance as he spoke, "How long have you been ill?"

"I have been this way for a month, but I am not ill."

"A month! Have you seen a doctor?"

She looked at him coolly. "No, and I do not need one. I am not ill. I assure you that it is nothing you can catch."

"I am more concerned that you need a doctor. How can you expect to get better on your own if you have already been sick a month?"

She stood staring at him for a while with a face of stone. Her lips pursed, and her face contorted into an ugly grimace before she answered, "It will all go away when I reach the second trimester."

His lips parted, but he did not speak. Where Jasmine was pale, color filled his cheeks. He thought back to their time in the boat, the scent of the canvas and the sound of the rain. "This is your third month?" She nodded. His eyes squinted in pain. He removed his cap and slapped it on his hip while looking down at the pool of vomit on the ground.

They endured the silence between them like a dull agony. Cleopatra whined in her master's arms. Joseph reached out and pet the cat behind its ears, and the animal purred. "Don't worry," he said.

Jasmine grinned sardonically. "Are you talking to me or the cat?"

He met her gaze. "What in the world are we going to do?"

"You mean, what am I going to do? What do you want me to do?"

He withdrew his hand from the hide of the cat and replaced his cap atop his head. "Can I get back to you on that?

"You can't tell me what you want me to do? Or are you afraid to ask?"

"I know what I want, but I don't know what is possible." He put his arm on her shoulder and leaned over and kissed her on the nose. "You'll forgive me for not kissing you on the lips."

Her smile matched his, and color returned to her cheeks as the tears welled up in her eyes and spilled over onto her face. “I love you, Joseph.”

Joseph pulled her face into his chest. “I know,” he said before he left.

Joseph 9

Phoenix

The source of the vision of the Phoenix Initiative came from an ancient legend, as do so many visions that serve as catalysts for humanity's grand scale achievements. The legend of Phoenix is a cautionary tale of a great city built in the midst of a vast desert, dependent on water diverted from far away rivers. In time, the human interventions required to maintain these artificial rivers failed the test of time, and the great city was returned to dust.

The legend serves to preach the timeless persistence of the forces of nature, and the folly of resisting its invulnerable tide. That the authors of the Phoenix Initiative themselves compared their creation to this mythical fiasco is testimony to their cynical desire to create an engine for wealth creation that would cease to function beyond their lifetimes.

—Book of History

When Joseph arrived at Port Augusto, his troops filed down the gangplank and formed two staggered arcs in a semicircle around their commander, the standard muster formation of the Roman Census.

"Stand tall!" Joseph commanded, bringing the men to attention. "Centurions, today we are in the shadow of the Valley of the Fallen. This is the edge of civilization, where the Nile Protocol is maintained through the force of arms. No one of us is prepared for the trials that lay before us. Warfare is not a craft learned through a lengthy apprenticeship. We will be tested early and often, and in the end it will be our fortitude and zeal that will determine our success more than our experience.

"We are green soldiers in a green land, and God loves all that is green." Chuckles emanated from the men despite strict conventions forbidding any sound or motion while in formation. "You will see people perish during your tour in this perimeter. Nothing can prepare you for that. Some of you will do the killing. Some of you could be among the killed. If one of you suffers torment after having killed, remember that, although terrible, it is still better to kill than to be killed."

A detail of centurions began transferring cargo from the *Terrier* to a team of pack mules. Joseph's company escorted the caravan. As soon as the cargo was off the boat, the *Terrier* set off downstream beneath a new moon that rendered it almost invisible at night. The only part of the hull easily seen was the portion previously beneath the waterline when the craft was fully loaded. This band of white now exposed appeared as a halo passing down the Blue Nile.

On board the crew toasted to another mission accomplished. On shore, the caravan of centurions and their herd headed off immediately to an inland destination unknown to anyone but their commander. Joseph reviewed his map one last time, committing the route to memory, then destroying the only written record known to reveal the location of the Phoenix mine shafts.

After a tortured journey through narrow passes on a moonless night, Joseph's caravan arrived at the well-graded plateau that housed one of history's most ambitious feats of engineering. At the base of the great derrick atop Mineshaft-One, the pack animals were led in a single file and their satchels removed from their backs, much to the tired animals' relief. The satchels were carried to an enclosure where a massive funnel burrowed deep into the earth. The satchels were opened for the first time, revealing their tremendous value to the carriers for a brief glimpse before being dumped into the darkness below. The shocked centurions froze at the sight of a fortune in diamonds being poured like water into the emptiness of the mine.

Steven

The lit fuse crackled and popped as it burned its way through a shallow trench. The trench was no deeper than a fist and the fuse the width of a finger. It ran in a more or less straight line for several hundred paces to the top of Mineshaft-One.

Steven might have been more attractive if he was not so overweight. As he knelt, his belly sagged almost to the ground. When he stood, neither his belt nor his suspenders could be trusted to hold up his pants against the weight of a gut that sagged over his waistline. "This will give us time to get over the ridge and take cover. Let's go," he said.

Jasmine threw her satchel over her back and joined him in a rapid march out of the valley. "Do these fuses ever burn faster than they are supposed to?" she asked.

His brow oozed perspiration, and he spoke only between labored breaths. "Almost never. They are quite reliable, really."

She increased her pace. "How far do you think we have to go to be clear of the debris?"

He panted words between gasps as they both neared a dead sprint. "The shrapnel will fill the whole valley. We need to clear the ridge. But don't worry, we have time."

They climbed the hillside a step at a time, no longer able to run up the incline. Sweat showed through their garments and dripped down their faces. When they cleared the ridge, they did not look back for fear the explosion would happen at any moment. They scurried down the slope on the other side of the ridge and found a shaded area below an outcropping of tall stones.

While they waited, Jasmine filled a tin with water and rested it on a flat portion of bedrock. She pulled Cleopatra from her satchel and set her beside the tin. The cat had just begun lapping the water when the explosion came.

The first sound to fill the air was a deafening concussion that was felt as much as it was heard. The impact of debris rattled across the valley on the other side of the ridge before silence reclaimed the area surrounding the blast.

Cleopatra burrowed into her satchel at the first report of the explosion. Jasmine went to gather her cat's water tin. She bent over and noticed the water in the pan was unsettled. The tiniest waves emanated from the center as though a pebble had been cast into the water. But instead of settling, these waves persisted, undiminished.

"Do you see this?" she called. "This bedrock is moving."

Steven nodded. "It is an earthquake."

"Because of the explosion?"

"Partly. This region is full of faults so earthquakes are bound to happen. When we explode the diamonds into these faults, it just speeds up the process."

"What is the sense in creating earthquakes?"

Steven shook his head from side to side. "I don't know what these explosions are for. My job is to go wherever I am asked and light the fuse."

Joshua

Black Market

The smuggling of Ethiopian coffee into the Nile watershed was an ancient practice dating to times before modern ethics prohibited such trade. Demand for the substance guaranteed a healthy margin for its suppliers. In their wisdom, the judges did their best to harness the wealth of the coffee market by creating a legal source that could launder illicit Ethiopian supplies.

In the higher elevations of the Upper Blue Nile watershed, along the Ethiopian frontier, coffee was cultivated under the auspices of the Nile Coffee Company. While ostensibly a private concern, the limited partners included a plethora of judges and other public officials, securing for itself privileged status.

The Roman Census itself was so manipulated for the benefit of the coffee monopoly. The official mission of the border patrol was to secure against smuggling and immigration between the two nations. However, the effect of its patterns of patrol served to channel all Ethiopian contraband through the territory controlled by the Nile Coffee Company. Ass by ass, the sacks of coffee came in and were emptied out of view of authorities into the bins of the warehouses perched in the highlands of the Blue Nile, a short stroll from the Ethiopian border. The laundering of Ethiopian coffee was known to few, obvious to most, but denied by all.

Ethiopian farmers in the highlands, where coffee cultivation and smuggling were part and parcel a way of life, belonged to two major factions. There were those known as loyalists, or "legals", who sold their produce to state authorities, and lived under the protective and coercive watch of the Ethiopian Regular Army. The other group, known as separatists, or "illegals", relied on the mysterious Northern Ethiopian Army to stave off the predatory ERA, which regularly raided the villages who dared to bring coffee directly to the insatiable Nile market, bypassing government authorities that depended on appropriating a portion of the lucrative trade to finance its downstream infrastructure. Both groups of farmers lived in fear of the other's military, for which brutality was the most common manner of competition.

Parallel to the ridgeline that was the border between the lands of the Blue Nile and Ethiopia wound a high, barely passable trail that, despite its difficult course, was traveled often by poachers, smugglers, and Centurions. When Centurions came across hapless trespassers in this no-man's-land, they seldom missed the opportunity to earn the bounty awarded for defending the deserts of the Roman Census.

Though poachers caught bearing arms in any part of a desert were summarily executed, the rules of engagement in the Alta Perimeter called for the death of any non-official personnel, armed or not. The dubious explanation for the creation of this free-fire-zone declared the typical excuses all militaries use to justify brute force against an outmatched opponent. Beneath the veneer of martial law, it was plain to all that the slaughter of those crossing the border in the regions patrolled by the Roman Census served to route contraband into the territory of the Nile Coffee Company, which was conspicuously absent of Centurions.

The castrated corpses of these victims of the border patrols hung in full view along this trail, dubbed the Ethiopian Way. The reward for a soldier presenting the scrotum of a trespasser was paid in the only hard currency of the day. And so it was said that the Ethiopian Way was paved with diamonds.

—Book of History

Sunset viewed from on high was to Joseph a religious moment. If nature was his religion, the lofty ridges of the Ethiopian Way were his cathedrals. A view devoid of man's interference with the natural world's state of affairs was reward enough for the daylong trek from the Alta Firebase to the outskirts of the Nile watershed high above. Here he could imagine his spirit unbridled by earthly concerns, free to join the effortless and timeless grace of the elements.

The men made camp at dusk, posting sentries on their perimeter, although the situation did not require such security. No one but no one engaged the Census in these parts. Inside the perimeter, a fire was lit, and the soldiers gathered around it, telling tales till they slept. The camaraderie lighted their spirits, and they dreamed of a victorious return to Khartoum and then onward to the new lands they had recently acquired.

Life presented itself as long, rich, and sweet in these days of star-filled skies and expanding vistas. If only other people's dreams could be half as sweet as their lives truly were. To think these soldiers of fortune were penniless vagrants not so long ago.

In the morning, Joseph unrolled a map of the area, weighting the four corners with stones to keep it from curling back into a cylinder. "This route is often traveled by smugglers," he spoke, tracing with his fingers along a trail on the map. "Here the path constricts between two points of high ground. All we need to do is get there, wait, and get lucky. Once they enter this canyon, there will be little they can do to defend themselves." His voice was calm and his face void of passion.

There was not even a whisper of dissent within the detachment once the order was given. Despite their lack of seasoning in the field, these men knew instantly that a call to arms was not subject to negotiation. Joseph paused briefly, stunned for a moment by the action materializing in response to his command. The men set out at a brisk pace, clearly exhilarated by the gravity of the task at hand. Poised at the brink of death, some would comment later that they never felt more alive.

A thin line of men passed through the canyon. They held no arms and walked leisurely, leaving little space between each other. All in all, they could not have conducted themselves in a manner making them any more vulnerable. When the last man of the group had entered the canyon, a forward observer raised a black flag to signal Joseph that no more men were to come.

He raised a horn to his lips without hesitation and then blew hard and long. His troops swarmed down on their prey. Both exits from the area were sealed while others came down from high ground on both sides of the pathway. Almost no resistance to the onslaught was given. Within a short time, the attackers had completely overpowered the hapless souls who had ventured into what would come to be known as "Joshua's Canyon."

A cry of celebration erupted that echoed through the valley. Relieved of their fear of the enemy, they now relished the prospect of reaping a hefty bounty for each of the fallen foes. The forward observers arrived at the scene first with the intent of performing the hasty post-mortem removal of scrota from the victims, as was standard operating procedure. Elation turned to awe as they went from corpse to corpse and found each was emaciated and already castrated. These were no guerrillas, and there would be no bounty.

"Commander, we have taken a prisoner."

"A man or a woman?"

"A man, but a castrated man only." The messenger believed the question of the gender of the captive pertained to the bounty that might be gained.

"Excellent. Take me to him at once." To Joseph, the mystery of the origin of the slain eunuchs ranked higher than a meager bounty. The messenger was perplexed by his commander's indifference towards the prisoner's bounty. Of what greater import might be this captured trespasser? What he did not know, he could not imagine. But Joseph was not typical in his thinking, and he readily fathomed the value at hand that was invisible to others around him.

This mentality of seeking to investigate was a strength in his role as a commander. It was the type of mindset that qualified him as a good candidate for greater responsibilities. In a system needing such leaders, he would thrive. In a system with a set command structure, his desire to acquire greater knowledge and the power that accompanies such knowledge would inevitably grate the nerves of the powers that be.

Joseph directed his messenger to lead him to the prisoner in his control, setting a course to learn information that would either make him welcome in the inner circle of his superiors, or feared as a rival in waiting. This was a course a man such as the messenger would never travel, even unintentionally. Joseph, on the other hand, could not resist the opportunity to satisfy his curiosity. And so the die was cast for one looking for more than what others meant to make known to him.

By the time Joseph arrived, his men had already transformed the captive from a man who felt lucky to be alive to one who was resigned to the fact that his death was imminent. All that remained in question was how much more agony he would have to endure in the limited time he had left. The interrogation could now proceed to its conclusion, where anything the inquisitor requested of the captive would readily reveal.

Joseph entered into the shrouded confines where his men had dutifully broken his body and mind. "What is your name, and where are you from?"

"Joshua, from Camp Abyei."

"Where is that?"

The man looked up at Joseph with amazement and laughed. "You do not know?"

"I will ask all the questions, and you will reply with only answers to these questions. Next time you fail to obey this order, I will take a break and you will remain here with my men until you are less obstinate. Clear?"

"Yes, sir. I meant no disobedience."

"Where is Camp Abyei?

"It is a day's stride from the border on the trail through this pass we are in now."

"Ethiopia!"

"Of course. You are the only Egyptians out here."

"What are you doing crossing into the Nile watershed from Ethiopia?"

Joshua shook his head in dismay. "What is the Nile watershed doing crossing into Ethiopia?"

Although Joseph had stated emphatically that the prisoner was not to pose questions of any kind under penalty of physical pain, he elected to pardon this man's offense. Joseph understood that in situations such as this, the power to permit a person to transgress could be more effective than the power to punish. Joseph directed his demands to his prisoner with a penetrating stare. "Tell me about Camp Abyei, how you came to this place, and why you fled."

Joshua relaxed, knowing now that his interrogator was not a sadist, but simply a man in search of information. "Loyalists removed us by force and concentrated us into Camp Abyei. This is a place where people die and nothing more. As dangerous as the path through the Alta Perimeter is, it is certain death to go any other way. Our hope was to reenter Ethiopia through the North Ethiopian checkpoint. Here we could find sanctuary and hope to resettle our land."

"You are a landowner? What land do you own?" A hint of mockery was obvious. This man had none of the characteristics of a gentleman.

"I am one of many who have claims to unsettled lands in the new frontier. By law, the government must open new frontier to all on a first come, first served basis. The government meant the land for their own purposes, so when droves of settlers arrived, it ruined their best-laid plans. Rather than let a horde of peasants stand in their way, they called us 'smugglers' and rounded us into camps."

Joseph gazed at the careworn face of a refugee and could not help but feel sympathy for a man in such dire straits that he freely risked his life rather than accept his current situation. "And you weren't smugglers?"

"Of course we were, everyone with an acre within a week's walk from the watershed border smuggles coffee into Egypt. It is far too lucrative a trade to take a back seat to meager edible crops."

"Tell me something I don't know. Tell me about this 'new frontier'."

"In the deserts at the lower elevations, the water table has risen to levels making it possible to sustain agriculture with irrigation. Rome released them to Ethiopia for harvesting."

Joseph paused for a moment of wonder. *New lands. The desert made to bloom. And just where it would be the most profitable. Such a brilliant scheme…* "How did you intend to reach the North Ethiopian checkpoint? And this time I want an answer with specifics."

Though Joshua was quick to answer every question posed to him by his captor, each answer only gave rise to more questions so that his interrogation stretched on through the evening. And despite the volume of information gathered, Joseph's report to the Census was brief to an extreme. Whatever intelligence he gathered was done so apparently for his own consumption.

When dawn broke, Joshua was allowed to view one last sunrise before his men led him away to his execution. As a warning to others that might venture into the Alta Perimeter, Joshua's carcass was affixed to a tree along the road, as was standard operating procedure. By the time the centurions had broken camp to begin their return to Fire Base Alta, birds were already circling above, and some had already landed in Joshua's tree. Still, no one witnessed the actual excarnation of Joshua, as the birds seemed to shy away from the corpse until the centurions had left the scene.

Mori

The Forger

Forgery, as much an art as a science, played an integral role in the life of Joseph and Jasmine. Ironically, one of the finest at the criminal craft found gainful employment for the judges behind the Phoenix Initiative. Mori, a repeat offender whose expertise at title fraud came to the attention of those close to the judiciary, was paroled under special conditions and assigned to the Nile Coffee Company for rehabilitation.

This arrangement provided the Phoenix Initiative the means to tie up loose ends that plague a crime of such magnitude. Facing interminable prison time should he reject the requests of his employer, he was considered perfectly reliable. His status as a convicted liar undermined his credibility to the extent needed to provide another attribute critical to the mission, namely that of deniability.

What was not foreseen, however, was the impact granting substantial power to a man living the life of a slave. Precautions taken to control the forger Mori perhaps raised a keen appreciation for liberty in a man whose life till then had always placed freedom of action above subordination to law, or any other sense of order.

Joseph and Jasmine would be beneficiaries of this man's enhanced skills and willingness to break the rules put in place by others who believed themselves his master.

—Book of History

Upon returning from the frontier, Joseph and his men reported to an unmarked building on the fringes of the command compound for a peculiar debriefing session. The men were taken individually behind a curtain and marked as would happen after consecrating a sacrament. This was recognition, they were told, for the execution of their solemn duties. The men accepted this version and were led to believe that this would all but exonerate them of their sins in the upcoming accounting. The only truth in all these rumors was that indeed these markings would determine the fate of Joseph's men in the Great Passover.

Joseph, a foreigner, did not require the mark his men received. Nevertheless, this venue proved fateful for Joseph as his first encounter with the author of the sacramental hieroglyphs, Mori the Fraud.

"Mori." Joseph spoke from within a canvas flap inside of a storage tent.

"Sir?" Mori responded, surprised to hear Joseph's voice come from the nondescript enclosure.

"Please enter without delay. I need to speak to you in private."

Mori entered. "Yes, sir. Can I be of service?"

"Perhaps. That is my hope, anyway. I must command your complete confidence in this matter, regardless of our meeting's outcome."

"That is the nature of my business. You can count on my silence, of course."

"Fine. That is excellent. You see, I am in the need of a forgery."

"Yes, well, I knew you weren't coming to me for crisis counseling."

Both men enjoyed a laugh at this remark. The humor helped warm their dialogue, sealing the relationship between two men so different only the clutches of their extreme circumstances could bond them together.

"For me to marry an Egyptian, I must be a virgin—or, that is, I must be able to prove it so." The term *virgin* meant in this context a man unable to bear children.

Joshua nodded, then removed his stenciling kit and began tattooing Joseph's inner forearm.

Jerome

Within the inner sanctum of the headquarters of Firebase Alta, the orderly room processed the endless series of legal documents necessary to conduct a military operation of such size and duration. Not that the workload was of much volume, but when something needed to be processed, an orderly was essential. Most of the time, though, the orderly sat at his desk and fought off boredom while others fought battles. Despite this lowly station, the orderly constituted the sole legal authority in the entire region. This power was bestowed by default, as any other qualified legal representative was nowhere to be found within days of the Alta Perimeter. With little else for which to claim any status whatsoever, the typical orderly personalized the importance of the law they oversaw and could be counted on to be sticklers for details.

Knowing all too well the fastidiousness of Jerome, the Alta Fire base orderly, Joseph prepared the case he was going to present with the thoroughness usually reserved for a high judgment. He walked into the untidy surroundings of Jerome's office with a satchel of documents to support his position. Joseph, hardly a legal scholar himself, benefited greatly from the assistance of Mori the Fraud. Mori, it seems, might have made a good lawyer, if only he lacked the desire to abide by the law he seemed to know all too well.

"Jerome, I have a request," Joseph said as he entered the presence of the orderly. His manner and tone conveyed the respect usually reserved by centurions for their superiors.

"Sir, I am at your service." For Jerome, these words were more than mere formality. For him, they were a creed.

"I need you to process a Life Status Change Order, and I am hoping it can be done quickly so that I may take leave afterwards."

"That will require certain documents to be in order, but if they are, it can be done in a quarter to half month."

"I have prepared all of the necessary documents on my end, but I need them processed today."

Jerome pushed away from his desk and straightened his posture. His face turned grave and quizzical as he looked Joseph square in the eye. "Are you speaking about a Life Status Change for yourself?"

"Yes. I intend to wed, and I wish to take leave afterwards."

Jerome's eyes blinked rapidly in nervous disbelief. "Sir, I am sure you are aware that a foreigner may not marry an Egyptian."

"Unless they qualify under an exception." Joseph produced a scroll referencing the paragraph in the Nile Protocol that had been attached to the orders that transferred him to Egypt.

Jerome read the paragraph indicated. "Sir, are you saying you are a virgin?"

At this, Joseph produced a second scroll, one that had been manufactured by Mori the Fraud. "I have my registration here."

Jerome did well to hide his surprise. He took the scroll, verified its authenticity to the best of his ability, then made note of the registration number on the marriage application in the "Special Circumstances" block.

"All you need now is a woman!"

Joseph replied to the proclamation with a laugh and a third scroll containing Jasmine's "Advice of Consent to Marry."

Jerome promptly notarized the marriage application, and with this, they were officially married.

"Thank you, Jerome. Now, I need you to issue me a pass for my honeymoon, beginning on our ceremonial wedding day."

"And when will this be, sir?"

"Tomorrow."

Jerome shook his head. "How am I supposed to grant you and Jasmine leave during Passover?"

Joseph produced another portion of the Nile Protocol, also from his special orders as a foreigner. "This states that as a foreigner, I may take leave during Passover expressly for the sake of a Life Status Change."

Jerome read the paragraph quickly. "That is fine for you, sir. But what about Jasmine?"

"She is my wife. Do you think the Protocol would make the provision permitting me to go on my honeymoon without taking my wife?" Joseph carefully straddled the line between a plaintiff before his judge and a commander issuing a browbeating.

Jerome did not answer. He reread the scroll containing the pertinent portion of the foreign officer's special orders. He labored to make sense of it all. "You are allowed to marry under the virginity exception. You are entitled to take leave for this Life Status Change. But the law does not directly cover your wife. How can I alleviate her of her legal obligations to participate in Passover?"

Joseph interjected before Jerome could finish his line of thought. "Does the provision for leave granted for Life Status Change explicitly exclude the case of marriage."

"Only playing devil's advocate, sir, but I imagine the Life Status Change envisioned by this exception was expected to involve a death of a parent or a similar event that would only concern the individual and not anyone else. Certainly not an Egyptian."

"You 'imagine'? But then why are there explicit terms by which I might marry an Egyptian woman?"

Jerome sat in silence. He was accustomed to filling out forms for a living. Sometimes this involved reading the fine print. Now, he would have to issue a judgment on competing portions of doctrine and law that he had never known to be in contradiction before. "If this were Khartoum, this case would be in a superior court."

"Jerome, we are a long ways from Khartoum. The only other document I can give you is this scroll with your wedding invitation inside of it. But I can't give it to you if you can't sign off on our honeymoon."

Jerome nodded and spoke apologetically. "Well, as a bachelor it might not be obvious to me, but I have to suppose that there's no law against having a bride accompany you on your honeymoon."

Joseph and Jasmine 5

True Love

Detractors of the New Nile made known through rumors a great many falsehoods about the marriage of Joseph and Jasmine that persist in the minds of many till the present. While it is a matter of discernable fact that Joseph did certainly engage the services of Mori the Fraud, there was no fraud in the sincerity of feelings between Joseph and Jasmine at the time of their marriage. Allegations that they had prior knowledge of the fate of the Blue Nile Tabernacle, and married only as a technique to avoid it cast doubt as to the virtue and courage of the pair.

For this reason, it is vital to understand that the purpose behind Joseph's solicitation of Mori to mark him a virgin was his determination to wed Jasmine for love's sake, with no prior knowledge of the perils their marriage would help them to avoid.

—*Book of Doctrine*

"Joseph and Jasmine, you have joined here today, in Fire Base Alta, to marry of your own free will. Your only intentions are to bring greater happiness to each other. May the purity of this union free your souls to love each other and never know loneliness again, for all eternity."

The couple stepped out from beneath the ceremonial awning suspended above them by their wedding party and endured the traditional wedding shower of grain seeds. They passed briskly through the gauntlet of well-wishers and then she was lifted by her wedding party up into the saddle of the awaiting ass. Joseph remained on foot and led the beast and his bride away from the enthusiastic salutations of the boisterous crowd.

The married couple would cherish the memory of this day not simply as the first day of their marriage, but also as the last day they would ever see their friends. The marriage of Joseph and Jasmine brought a time of rejoicing to the usually quiet firebase in its last month of existence. In the tents and the narrow passages between them, all felt an air of vitality. It is almost impossible not to share the emotions of comrades in close quarters, where sharing is the rule and solitude the exception.

In these, the fading days of this wilderness outpost, an exchange took place between the bride and groom and their wedding guests. The men of Joseph's company and the coworkers of Jasmine would take away feelings of mirth that would resonate in their hearts for the brief remainder of their lives. Jasmine and Joseph would take with them the memories of those whose assailants meant to be forgotten.

THE BOOK OF THE GREAT PASSOVER

(This passage follows Atonement)

Izzi 4

Accounting

The doors would not open until the third day. On the first day, the Day of Atonement, the tellers took their places in the confessionals, and received the people one by one. It was the task of the tellers to collect particular information from individuals that would feed into the Weighted Rubric. Sins of all kinds were recorded. Most sins were a matter of record, and so much of the time the process simply involved the teller verifying a person's identity.

Birthmarks tattooed at an infant's baptism were matched with the temple ledger. Other hieroglyphs were tattooed for other sacraments. Marriage, parenting, virginity, abortion, death of a child, and all things concerning one's potential impact on the population of the Nile were subtly encrypted on the forearms of people so that the Passover Festival could conform the nation to God's will.

During the all day process of accounting, clerics continuously burned incense that released opiates into the temple atmosphere. This helped the parishioners cope with their anxieties, which in turn facilitated the tellers in their special actions.

—Book of Mysteries

Now locked within the Blue Tabernacle for the duration of the Passover, the congregation filed into the confessional one at a time. "Please state your name," an anonymous voice asked from behind a wooden lattice that masked his identity.

"Izzi." He tugged on his beard nervously.

"And your place of birth?"

"The Upper Nile Reserve."

"Current home of record?"

"Khartoum."

"Your profession?"

"Soldier of the Roman Census."

"Any children born to you, and their genders?"

"None."

"Any sacraments received in the last year?"

"Yes." Izzi put forward his forearm, revealing the tattoo placed there by Mori the Fraud.

Behind the woodwork the scratching sound of a stencil filled the silence of the confessional. Then the scratching came to an end. "That is all. Pray for God's mercy for your sins."

And this process was repeated for each and every person in the Nile watershed as it had been done so many times before in years past. The populace was accustomed to such a routine to the extent that hardly a soul questioned its place in the overall scheme of things.

Day of Marking

The Day of Marking was one of the most sensitive operations of the entire Passover process. After accountings were submitted to the Weighted Rubric, a person's fate was encrypted into a temporary marking. Only a few in the Census and clergy could decipher the marks, and this was done at the moment of assignment. This left individuals with no inkling of how they had fared in the rolling of the draedles until completely powerless to resist. As each person was led down the darkened tunnels to their assigned billet the aroma of the opiate-rich incense was thick in the stagnant air. Many succumbed to the fumes, and rested peacefully through Easter eve.

—Book of Mysteries

Easter

Everywhere in temples large and small elite guards began the ultimate phase of the Passover celebration by channeling water from the baptismal pools into reservoirs above the billets housing the congregation below.

When the water rose to a given depth the guards untied the sacred scroll, which identified which of the ceramic seals would be released to allow water to flood the billet below, drowning all within. Even the sounds of their death screams were drowned by the rushing water, so that the survivors slept through the night listening to the water pass over.

—*Book of Mysteries*

Izzi 5

Izzi strained to keep his eyelids open as opium continued to fill the air. He was led from the temple's main atrium to a descending hallway that led in turn to a series of rooms below the baptismal lagoon. A temporary marking on his forehead determined which of these rooms would house him during the final act of Passover. On one door was a larger version of the marking on his forehead, and here the ushers directed Izzi to enter.

The ushers did the same for everyone in the congregation, and when they were finished, they bolted shut all the doors to the rooms from the outside hallway. When the bolt slid shut to the room where Izzi had been led, he looked around to find the entire contingent of his company housed alongside him. The semi-random manner of marking and accounting made such a coincidence a statistical impossibility. All within the room quickly realized they had been collocated intentionally. "We will all be spared," Izzi foretold. This prediction was repeated until a buzz permeated the room.

The ushers assembled around the altar where the chaplain issued each of them a scroll with a list of symbols. These symbols could also be found on the doors to the rooms beneath the baptismal lagoon, as well as on the foreheads of the faithful within the rooms.

"This is the will of God," he said to each of his ushers as he handed them their scroll.

From the atrium, the ushers ascended a spiral staircase leading to the crawl space below the lagoon and above the rooms now housing the congregation. This space housed a network of pipes filled with water from the lagoon. Above each room there was a valve marked with a symbol, the same as the symbol on the door of the room below.

One usher approached a valve identified by a simple cross within a circle. Finding this same symbol on his scroll, he proceeded to turn a wheel, opening the valve. Izzi had just succumbed to the opium fumes and was resting quietly despite the din of his comrades celebrating their good fortune. He awoke when the din turned instantly to silence. His eyes opened to see water pouring into the room from a vent in the ceiling. None of Joseph's company would survive the Great Passover.

THE BOOK OF THE NEW NILE

Joseph and Jasmine 6

Accompanied by Joseph, her newlywed husband, Jasmine strode across the level ground surrounded by hillsides that echoed their every word. They were perfectly comfortable in each other's presence, and they had no greater desire than to share one another's company.

She sat on the edge of the crater that used to be the top of Mineshaft-Two and looked at the clouds building far away to the north.

"It looks like we may be in for a shower!"

"When it rains, it pours," he said, smiling, as if there was something comical in the phrase.

"That's what they say," she responded, also smiling.

He drew her close to him, and the two kissed. They held each other in a silence that was timeless, a pure and endless moment when the world around them dissolved into oblivion, leaving them alone to occupy each other's hearts and minds.

The rain began suddenly and with fury. It was all he could do to keep his general-issue rain tarp from blowing away while it was wrapped around them both as they huddled in a crouch. The tempest persisted, and soon arroyos in the surrounding foothills filled with water and headed gushing to the plain in which they stood. Within minutes, the plain turned into a shallow lake. They climbed onto a boulder the same height as a man and huddled together while the water rose to within an arm's length of where they took refuge.

She trembled in fear as the water rose. He calmed her with assuring words, "It is only a shallow pond. The water is not moving. If we have to, we can swim to the hillside and climb above the waterline."

But the water did not rise further. It was at this moment that she realized how flat the surrounding land was and how the water did not seem to be moving in any direction. As a keen hydrologist, she could not see how so much water could gather here and yet not rise. Even stranger, before the rain had completely ended, the water began to recede. It continued to lower, until the ground around them was again void of standing water. She stepped off the boulder and noticed the drop-off was a full step more than before the rain.

"The plain has subsided!" she spoke in tremors. "All the water has gone into Mineshaft-Two! Where is it going from there?"

"The same place we are," Joseph said.

Baltazar 1

North Ethiopia

The official purpose for legitimizing the rebel border was to keep coffee smugglers from crossing into Egypt, in an attempt by the Census to regulate by diplomacy what it could not through force. For the North Ethiopian Army the border helped to stem the flow of weapons into Ethiopia to their enemies. The agreement to settle the border was, as often is the case with borders, due to exhaustion on both sides from contesting the ownership of a disputed territory. Even still, the frontier between Egypt and North Ethiopia was tenuous at best, and never amounted to more than a line of control between warring parties.

—Book of History

From a ridge, he could see the North Ethiopian Army's checkpoint. Because he knew a centurion was as likely as not to be slaughtered on sight by the troops that maintained this stronghold, he kept his distance. Removing a set of semaphores from a satchel, Joseph signaled his credentials as a messenger carrying the will of Joshua. Signals were returned that he could approach the checkpoint under a cease-fire.

The guards were surprised to see a centurion accompanied by a woman. They were familiar with the hardened hearts of those who hunted people like animal prey. The fact that he came bearing personal effects communicated that he did not deny the humanity of his foe. With Jasmine at his side, the guards looked on them both as guests rather than sworn enemies worthy of contempt and violence. They and their animals were offered shade and water. In kindness, he presented them with a bottle of spirits from his days in Aswan. Nestled high above the rivers that divided these people to the point of warfare, both sides enjoyed a respite from the hatred of these times that engulfed almost everyone involved in misery.

"Is it permissible for me to accompany this will to the officials who need to see it?"

The guards, perhaps becoming accustomed to the novelties of this strange encounter, were slow to dismiss him. Nevertheless, they knew of no way to accommodate such a bold request. "All we can say is that such contact is against our most specific orders not to disclose the location of our leaders to the Census. You will have to leave Joshua's will with us."

"I have sworn to deliver it directly," Joseph replied. "Is it possible your leaders could send an emissary?"

Obviously moved by a stranger's commitment to one of their fallen comrades, they huddled briefly and then gave their response, "We are only low-ranking guards, but we will find a way to help you."

Led blindfolded along twisting mountain passes, Joseph and Jasmine arrived at the North Ethiopian headquarters completely disoriented. The scent of canvas mixed with the equally strong aroma of coffee. "Remove their blindfolds," an older man's voice commanded.

Baltazar, general of the rebels, looked into the eyes of his guest as a preliminary greeting. "Welcome to North Ethiopia." He handed each fruit, completing the customary three-part greeting common in these lands.

"You are a gracious host," Jasmine replied. Her upbringing gave her natural insight into such traditions, and her host smiled with pleasure at her humble response. Jasmine then looked sideways at Joseph, communicating to him to follow her lead.

"Yes. Nice place. Smells like you folks have plenty of coffee around here," Joseph offered. Jasmine shook her head in amused dismay.

Baltazar raised his eyebrows. "I don't live in this tent, my friend. It is only a temporary shelter for which I hold no sentimental value." His smile left his face.

"Nevertheless, you have brought us to a place far nicer than where we have been billeted lately," Jasmine said, digging her nail into her husband to force him into silence.

A grin returned to Baltazar's face. "Please be seated," he said as he gestured towards a pair of canvas chairs. He seated himself after his guests. "I wish to thank you for bringing to us the will of Joshua. He made extensive claims in these parts and so there could be considerable confusion over its possession after his passing."

"I have always been a strong believer that everyone has a responsibility for the future. A will is an important part of anyone's legacy."

"Yes, I couldn't agree more." The general hunched forward, as if what he had to say next required physical exertion. "Of course deeding one's land is never as easy as drawing up a will. Unfortunately, affairs concerning land are more complicated in North Ethiopia. Those of us outside of the downstream circle of judges are at a supreme disadvantage in their legal system. Most who file claims with federal officials find themselves corralled into refugee camps by the local constabulary on some trumped-up charge."

"Such as smuggling," Joseph interrupted, a hint of condescension embedded in his question.

Baltazar took no insult in his words. "Smuggling, poaching, tax evasion—a whole arsenal of misdemeanors that the constabulary reserves the right to apply as it sees fit. It is not that we refute such crimes. Such things are accepted norms in North Ethiopia. But the constabulary enforces these laws that no one follows against those at odds with the judges, solely. Collaborators are conspicuously absent from the rolls of internment centers."

Jasmine's eyes widened with every revelation. Joseph's face took on a pained look. "These smugglers that the Census chases in the Alta Perimeter, do they include collaborators?"

"No, of course not." Baltazar's reply verged on ridicule. "What do you smell in this tent?"

"Coffee."

"Yes. That is our business. We smuggle coffee. We all smuggle coffee. The only question is, how? Collaborators pay export tariffs to the judges, and the constabulary provides them secure access to the Nile Coffee Company. The rest of us go direct to the Nile marketplace, which means we have to avoid the constabulary and the Census."

"I am aware of the Census's role in preventing smuggling, but how are we of any assistance to these collaborators?"

Baltazar unrolled a map and laid it flat on a table. "It is simple. Look where the Census patrols on the Nile side of the border. Your patrols end here, on the border, where the Ethiopian constabulary patrols begin. It is all one operation. To get coffee to the Nile from Ethiopia, you have two choices: deal with the constabulary or avoid the Census."

Joseph leaned backwards into the canvas back of his chair, lifting the front legs off the ground, then leaned forward to touch them down again. "You seem to be saying that a man's dying wish carries less weight than those of the living."

"This concern of yours for this man's will is remarkable. I haven't found honor to be a motivation among the Census. If I didn't know better, I would guess that your true intention was to gather intelligence on our operations."

Jasmine's eyes dilated briefly, recognizing the manner of speech expressed that Baltazar suspected Joseph of spying. Joseph saw the gravity of the allegation made through such a suggestion. "You need not worry, General. I have no intention of returning to Egypt. In fact, maybe you would find it in your interest to grant my wife and I asylum here in North Ethiopia."

Again, Jasmine's eyes dilated, and a shudder passed down her spine.

Baltazar blinked twice, stunned by his guest's petition. "Do what?"

"My thinking is this batch of coffee about to rot in this tent might be more valuable if a centurion were available to show you how to navigate through the Alta Perimeter."

Baltazar's eyebrows rose in interest, while Jasmine's mouth opened in awe. "If you are willing to provide such assistance, I assure you the reward would be most handsome. What do you require as a retainer?"

"For starters, a cup of coffee would be nice."

Baltazar smiled. "Forgive my rudeness for not offering you it earlier, Joseph. Jasmine, how do you take your coffee?"

A messenger burst into the tent full of words and short of breath. "The Census is gone. The Census is gone," he blurted between gasps for air.

The general stood and offered his exhausted soldier his chair. "Relax, young man. Tell me what you mean by this."

The messenger seated himself and recovered to the point where he could speak in a calm voice. "There are no patrols on the border. There are no troops in Fire Base Alta. No one at all in the whole perimeter has been seen since Passover."

Joseph, Jasmine, and Baltazar exchanged looks of amazement. Baltazar nodded his head repeatedly back and forth. "Joseph, what do you know of this?"

After a short delay, he replied, "If there is no one in the Fire Base, then there can be only two possibilities: either they have been evacuated or they perished in the Passover."

"All of them?" Jasmine cried.

Joseph took her hand while looking at Baltazar. "Both cases are strange, but the latter is the most likely."

"Either way, no centurions are in the perimeter?"

"Reinforcements will arrive. But for now, no."

"Messenger, take this message to my lieutenants."

"Yes, sir."

"Rally all of our men at the checkpoint, plus five thousand strides west."

The messenger paused and revealed his shock at this command by stammering a hesitant "Yes, sir" again before leaving. Five thousand strides west of the checkpoint was inside the Nile watershed and also within the Alta Perimeter.

Joseph 10

The general leaped in a single bound atop a rock that gave him a full view of the men assembled before him. The soldiers who had been mulling inquisitively amongst themselves gave their attention to their leader. "It has become apparent that a window of opportunity has arisen for us to pass through the Alta Perimeter unchallenged by the Roman Census. Our goal in this brief period is to make safe passage along the Ethiopian Way until we reach the pass leading to the Abyei internment center.

"Here we intend to take high ground to the west of the camp in support of a subsequent strike against the unprotected western wall of the camp defenses. Once we have penetrated the outer wall, our superior numbers will make further defense of this facility an exercise in futility for our opponent.

"Double rations have been issued. You will only require one ration a man, at most. You are carrying the second ration for the sake of feeding our countrymen interned in the center, many of whom are starving to death on the diet provided by their captors. It is as important that we liberate them from hunger as from bondage."

Baltazar turned the men over to his lieutenants, who immediately marched them west into a setting sun, deeper and deeper into Egypt. Joseph led the Emancipation Brigade of the NEA from their checkpoint, through the Alta Perimeter, and into the same pass where Joshua had been caught fleeing in the opposite direction. He brought his troops to rest in the shade of the tree where Joshua had been hung. There were no signs of the man, which was most unusual. The birds had carried him away, bones and all.

Here, Joseph addressed his men in reverent tones. "This is the tree upon which Joshua hung. He died that others might live. Today, we live that others might not die."

The Emancipation Brigade crossed into the highlands above Camp Abyei without being detected, let alone contested. The Ethiopian Regular Army had always depended on the Census to defend the Egyptian approaches to this encampment. Nothing then prevented the swift takeover of the tactical key terrain necessary to seize the lightly fortified outpost. In short order, the camp was liberated by troops in the command of Baltazar under the banner of North Ethiopia.

Even these carefree soldiers of fortune felt sullen and filled with sympathy for the survivors of the camp they found malnourished and disease ridden. Furthermore, the men had been castrated almost without exception. Initially the liberators fed them a diet of broth, as anything more solid might bring them dysentery.

After the first supper of their liberation, Joseph rose before the survivors and gave a most solemn address. "I rise and speak before you all on behalf of Joshua, known to you all, but gone from us now. I do so not to honor him, but to bury him, because I am certain his soul cannot rest until his will be known to you. As executor of his will, I assure you I will not rest until all of you are made beneficiaries of the sacrifice Joshua made." He opened a scroll and read the preamble, "'With God as my witness, I submit this will, and I do so under terms that are freely accepted…'"

Lansing 2

Let justice be done, though the world perish.

—Emperor Ferdinand I

During the days following the Great Passover, the Khartoum probate court labored over the caseload that dramatically increased every year at this time. In this year, the court found itself inundated with estate settlements, the volume of which exceeded any before. All people living upstream of Khartoum who fell in the Great Passover were processed in this court where the inhabitants of the Upper Nile were reduced by half.

The crush of the workload made for hasty work, as temporary clerks processed parish after parish with speed unknown to a system of laws. When the estates of the Blue Nile were settled, it was determined that a full eighty percent had perished. "There must be a drought forecast that exceeds all others," he murmured as the tallies came in. Still, no one suspected the legitimacy of the ritual, and revolt against it remained only a distant notion.

Judge Lansing scarcely looked at the settlements prepared by the clerks before signing off on them. But when the bundle of paperwork for the sacrifice of the Blue Nile Tabernacle was placed on his desk, he looked at the twine that bound them and recalled the peculiar filing of these centurions earlier in the year. He called the clerk of Khartoum to the bench. "This is the group of recruits with the land holdings, isn't it?"

The clerk glanced at the pile, then looked up casually before replying, "Yes, I recognize these men's names from the research you assigned to me."

"I want you to do some more research. This pile tells me how many died. I want to know how many lived."

The pilot of the *Terrier* was escorted into the chambers of Khartoum's judge of probate by both a sheriff and a centurion. This show of force by both the local and global authority was unusual for a civil proceeding. There was no mistaking the gravity of matters under consideration. Authorization from Rome was required for a centurion to be involved in a local case.

When the judge arrived, he took his seat slowly behind his large oak desk. He addressed his sheriff first, "This is the pilot of the boat seized yesterday, I presume?"

"Yes, Your Honor. And here is your subpoena for the same." The sheriff handed the judge a scroll bound by a red ribbon.

"Your Honor," the pilot spoke in plaintiff tones.

"Yes, pilot."

"May I view this subpoena that has been served to me?"

"No such luck, pilot. This and all other documents of concern to this case are hereby sealed under the diplomatic secrecy standard of the Nile Protocol and the House of Law."

The captain was clearly intimidated by this announcement. He could divine from the probate judge's opening remarks that as long as he was in Khartoum, he was at the mercy of local authority.

"Pilot, your vessel has been seized as bond against the Nile Coffee Company, which we know to be the actual owner of the *Terrier*. Furthermore, the Nile Coffee Company has admitted to this court that you are the lead agent in the transactions that promised land grants to the deceased centurions who perished in the Blue Nile Tabernacle in the recent Passover. Do you deny your role in these transactions between your company and these men?"

The pilot, as was his option, remained silent in the face of this line of questioning. Assertions by the bench, while phrased as questions, were actually rhetorical. Refuting the opinion of a judge was a futile defense and could bring contempt charges if the presiding judge was in a punitive mindset.

"Let the record show the witness confirms this fact with his silence," the judge continued. "These men's estates are due the titles to these lands as per the contracts entered into here in Khartoum, as registered with the clerk of Khartoum. Is this understood?"

"Your Honor, it is not clear at all how the estates of these centurions who died while stationed in the provinces of the Blue Nile Tabernacle can be determined here in Khartoum."

"All of these men established their estates in Khartoum the day they enlisted. The fact that they died somewhere else is of no consequence to the determination of the jurisdiction of their probate settlement."

That so many men had been able to navigate the bureaucracy of Khartoum so quickly, in less than a day, confounded him. No attorney with less than a boatload of diamonds could receive such preferred treatment. "How did these men register their estates in such short order?"

The judge signaled the centurion who had escorted the captain to speak. "They filled out beneficiary forms that were in their enlistment package and had it signed by the officer that swore them into the Census."

The pilot was not an attorney, but he was still very quick on his feet. "If these men registered their estates with the witness of a centurion and with a Census form, isn't this a matter for the Census to decide?"

Again, the judge gestured to the attending centurion, who said, "The Census declines to take on a role as a party of any kind in this affair. It is the decision of Rome that this matter of the estates of these centurions be determined by this court." It was clear the Census wished to abandon its partnership in this initiative in the hopes that its role might not be disclosed.

The pilot was frustrated, but desperate not to concede. "This witness should be included in these proceedings. How else can forgery be ruled out?" Having left Fire Base Alta prior to the marriage of

Joseph and Jasmine, the pilot assumed both had perished in the Blue Nile Tabernacle.

"Forgery. Well, that might explain the fact that until recently the lands deeded to the men of this lost company belonged to a number of judges in the Delta. As for the beneficiary forms, Captain Joseph has confirmed that he witnessed these forms in writing. This confirmation came via diplomatic pouch from Ethiopia," the judge of probate replied.

"North Ethiopia," the centurion offered.

"I stand corrected, thank you. Are there any other comments for this court?"

This time the pilot was speechless.

"Very well. I hereby designate Jasmine of *North Ethiopia* the rightful owner of the properties promised by the Nile Coffee Company to the centurions who perished in the Blue Nile Tabernacle. Praise be to God." The jurist bowed his head and held the room silent as he prayed to himself. After a while, he looked up again and looked towards the clerk. "Now, let us dispense with the other matter at hand."

The pilot bristled while the clerk read the heading of the next case before the court, "*Nile vs. The Nile Coffee Company.*"

The judge spoke without notes, directing his undivided attention on the pilot of the *Terrier*. "How can this court but conclude that the Nile Coffee Company provided downstream judges every assurance that these lands would never be stripped from their possession? How can any reasonable person believe the land proffered these dead centurions was done so in good faith?"

The pilot looked back into the eyes of the judge leering down at him from his bench. "Your Honor, this is purely circumstantial."

"Circumstance with motive. A company of men is promised land they can never expect to own. The same company, in its entirety, perishes in the most recent Passover, leaving no one to possess the lands promised them. How do you explain this unlikely scenario without malice and fraud being involved?"

"Your Honor, the Nile Coffee Company held title to these lands and made them the legal property of these men. There is no crime in this."

"No crime! These men are dead at the hands of an ungodly plot!"

"They perished in the Passover by an act of God."

"That is absurd and tantamount to blasphemy. The Blue Nile Passover has obviously been corrupted as part of this scheme. Of greater consequence than the fraud perpetrated in this land deal is the manipulation of our religious institutions for insidious special interests. What is your role in all of this?"

"I just run a boat, Your Honor. I take people and boats where I am told to take them."

"But I suspect you know a good deal about those who tell you where to go and what to do. I can spare you punishment if you cooperate with the investigation of this matter."

The pilot shook his head from side to side. Sweat beaded on his naked scalp. "Your Honor, I have nothing left to say."

The judge gestured for the bailiff to approach. "You are to be held in irons until such time when you have more to say." He leveled his gavel with such force the handle split in half.

Baltazar 2

Jerod wore the ankle-length black robe of an Egyptian diplomat despite the unbearable heat of the afternoon sun. Late spring in Ethiopia was a difficult time to acclimatize to higher elevations, where the rebels made their headquarters. Inside a canvas tent, he found relief from the sun, but had to endure the oppressive heat in a room where the air was stifled by the windowless walls.

"Welcome to North Ethiopia," Baltazar greeted Jerod with his palms open, gesturing him to take a seat. Jerod kept his hands tucked within his robe and sat himself without responding. "Can I offer you something to drink?"

"Water," Jerod half-gasped. Almost before he had said the word, a filled glass was provided. He took it and drank it at once, spilling a few drops at the corners of his mouth in his haste. From within his robe, he produced a scroll tied with a black ribbon. "My credentials, sir."

Baltazar took the scroll and read it to himself. "Your arrival is earlier than we had expected. I assume you wish to proceed with the matters at hand."

"Precisely so. The matter of Jasmine's inheritance is of immediate concern."

"Understood. And we, of course, hope to do everything we can to reconcile our countries' differences." Baltazar passed him a scroll of his own, also tied with black ribbon.

When Jerod finished reading it, he looked up at his opposite. "I am empowered to accept these terms if I can be assured that Jasmine never exercises her claims to the lands left her in Egypt."